John Irving's Existentialist Heroes

An Analysis

by Mathias Sajovitz

Contents

1. Introduction

> Like a good writer, who must love and worry each detail, Jenny Garp would spend hours noticing the habits of a single human cell. Like a good writer, she was ambitious; she hoped she would get to the bottom of cancer. In a sense, she would. She would die of it.
>
> Like other doctors, Jenny Garp took that sacred oath of Hippocrates, the so-called father of medicine, wherein she agreed to devote herself to something like the life Garp once described to young Whitcomb—although Garp was concerned with a *writer's* ambitions ("… trying to keep everyone alive, forever. Even the ones who must die in the end. They're the most important to keep alive"). Thus, cancer research did not depress Jenny Garp, who liked to describe herself as her father had described a novelist.
>
> "A doctor who sees only terminal cases."
>
> In the world according to her father, Jenny Garp knew, we must have energy. Her famous grandmother, Jenny Fields, once thought of us as Externals, Vital Organs, Absentees, and Goners. But in the world according to Garp, we are all terminal cases. (Garp 608-609)

The above quoted passage can be seen as an indication of what the analysis at hand is going to deal with: an existentialist analysis of the absurd human existence as portrayed by John Irving.

Often referred to as a master of the absurd, John Irving has without a doubt succeeded in portraying life in its 'essence,' which according to him is: confusing, cruel, unfair and at the same time a source of amusement. When someone acquainted with existentialist philosophy reads Irving's novels *The Water-Method Man*, *The Hotel New Hampshire* and *The World According to Garp*, it will be hard for them not to be tempted to view Irving's writing through an existentialist lens.

Although Irving's novels can be meaningfully interpreted from an existentialist perspective, I was surprised to find that no interpretation of Irving's writing has been attempted with this particular focus in mind. Scholarly literary criticism on John Irving appears to have restricted itself to narrative criticism, not paying attention to a particular school of thought. In my opinion, however, John Irving's characters can best be understood—besides the rather obvious ironic and absurd narrative twists and turns—in a really meaningful context, only when analyzing their attitudes, behaviors and actions within a particular framework; one that existentialism appears to be able to provide. All of Irving's protagonists who are dealt with in this analysis are "disoriented individual[s] facing a confused world that [they] cannot accept" (Solomon, From Hegel 238), which marks the beginning of the existentialist attitude. Given the *Bildungsroman*-like structure of some of Irving's novels, it is tempting to argue that the plots encountered in this analysis deal with the protagonists' adjustments to living in an absurd world.

Literary critics have acknowledged this existentialist role in making Irving's characters important and appealing. However, to date they have not established a thorough framework in which all existentialist aspects of Irving's writing would come together.

The aim of the analysis at hand is to refer to existentialist philosophy as such a framework, through which it should become possible to successfully attempt a breakdown of Irving's protagonists' lives in an absurd world and demonstrate that the narrative and the characters follow an existentialist pattern. By doing so, the analysis will aim to demonstrate that most of John Irving's protagonists can be seen as existentialist heroes per se and that their behavior and their actions could subsequently be referred to as existentialist exploits.

Existentialism as a literary framework for the analysis of John Irving on the one hand can, in my opinion be justified, as the protagonists' lives and attitudes are reminiscent of existentialist personae in search of meaning, who do not involve themselves in metaphysical reasoning. Rather, these existentialist heroes are conscious or in the process of becoming aware of their awkward human state in a world shaped by absurdity and find their own ways, and their own moralities to deal with it. Moreover, it has to be noted that it was the American novel, which exercised significant influence on existentialism as such. Existentialism and the French existentialist novel in depicting life in its concreteness, particularity and verity in fact needed the American novel with its "attacks and devices" (Bruneau 66) as an influence. It thus makes perfect sense to relate existentialism and postmodern American literature. Assuming an existentialist nature of American literature thus would allow for the analysis of many other American authors. Clearly, the work of T.C. Boyle—whose mentor at the University of Iowa Writers Workshop was John Irving—would allow for an existentialist analysis. Norman Mailer is a prominent example of an American writer, who would actually claim to be existentialist. Gore Vidal, with his taboo breaking works, or E.L. Doctorow—who himself once stated he "trust[ed] the existentialist vision" (Friedl and Schulz 183)—represent two other important American authors whose work could be seen from an existentialist perspective.

The analysis comprises three parts. In the first part, I intend to create the context for an analysis of an existentialist hero. Particularly the works of Jean Paul Sartre and Albert Camus will be outlined in order to create a framework. Both of these existentialist writers approach life as an event, which has no deeper meaning and which cannot be understood by an individual human being in terms of metaphysics. Existentialist philosophy only allows for one truth: that all we can know for sure is that we exist. Anything beyond our own existence is speculation and subsequently not relevant for how we lead our lives. This ultimately leads to the conclusion that only the individual human being can judge his own deeds and morality. However, by giving priority to existence over metaphysical essence, existentialism creates an enormous amount of individual freedom. At the same time, this subsequently imposes a lot of responsibility on individuals and implies the existence of many a trap that can prevent an individual to live fully and authentically. Ultimately, humans are condemned to freedom: excuses are not an option. Self-determination of personal actions leads to the assumption that only people themselves can give their lives meaning. This culminates in Sartre's statement that "[m]an is not the sum of what he has already, but rather the sum of what he does not yet have, of what he could have." The outline of

Camusean and Sartrean existentialism provides the point of departure for defining this analysis' existentialist hero.

In the second part, the analysis at hand will apply existentialism to the three before mentioned novels written by John Irving, and examine the extent to which the characters portrayed fulfill the role of existentialist heroes.

Part three will conclude this analysis by tying up loose ends and conducting an evaluation of the degree of existentialism that can be found in Irving's work.

Ultimately, I hope to succeed in demonstrating that Irving's novels are a mirror of existentialist ways of living, and that one can get a deeper and more holistic understanding of John Irving when reading him through an in-depth existentialist lens.

2. Towards An Existentialist Framework

2.1. An Outline of Jean-Paul Sartre's Philosophy

Jean Paul Sartre (1905-1980) created his branch of existentialism under the influence of Edmund Husserl, Georg Wilhelm Friedrich Hegel and Martin Heidegger. It is thus no surprise at all that crucial parts of his thought are connected to phenomenology (phainómenon = "that which appears," lógos = study, idea), a philosophical movement which tries to gain knowledge about the world through its manifestations. In phenomenological perspective, reality cannot be understood as an autonomous occurrence, but only be "thought" through human consciousness.

In his core work *Being and Nothingness* Sartre examines human existence through a phenomenological ontological perspective, and divides *being* into three categories: *being-in-itself* (être-en-soi), *being-for-itself* (être-pour-soi) and *being-for-others* (être-pour-autrui). While *being-for-itself* can only exist through the human mind, *being-in-itself* is independent from human consciousness. *Being-for-itself* thus *is* the human consciousness, *being-in-itself* subsequently represents everything which is transcendent to the mind, such as the objects of the external world.

Sartre explains that

> Consciousness is the revealed-revelation of existents, and existents appear before consciousness on the foundation of their being. Nevertheless the primary characteristic of the being of an existent is never to reveal itself completely to consciousness. An existent can not be stripped of its being; being is the ever present foundation of the existent; it is everywhere and nowhere. (Being and Nothingness 24)

Being-in-itself does neither depend on a relation to itself nor to the outer world, cannot transcend itself and is neither active nor passive, Nothingness does not exist in *being-in-itself*. Nothingness comes into place only in conjunction with the mind, since consciousness allows for negation. The human mind receives input, allowing for relating itself to the outer world. However, passive reception is impossible for the human mind, as being conscious also implies to shape our realities. It is this interplay within the human mind that allows for Nothingness to become a given:

> Nothingness is *not*. If we can speak of it, it is only because it possesses an appearance of being, a borrowed being, as we have noted above. Nothingness is not, Nothingness "is nihilated." It follows therefore that there must exist a Being (this can not be the In-itself) of which the property is to nihilate Nothingness, to support in its being, to sustain it perpetually in its very existence, *a being by which nothingness comes to things*. [...] The Being by which Nothingness arrives in the world is a being such that in its Being, the Nothingness of its Being is in question. *The being by which Nothingness comes to the world must be its own Nothingness.* (Sartre, Being and Nothingness 57-58)

In order to exemplify the occurrence of Nothingness and its being contingent on the mind (*being-for-itself*), Sartre uses the example of himself looking for his friend in a café, where they were supposed to meet:

> But now Pierre is not here. This does not mean that I discover his absence in some precise spot in the establishment. In fact Pierre is absent from the *whole* café; his absence fixes the café in its evanescence; the café remains *ground*; it persists in offering itself as an undifferentiated totality to my only marginal attention; it slips into the background; it pursues its nihilation. (Sartre, Being and Nothingness 42)

This analogy exemplifies the key idea of existentialism as such: That existence precedes essence. In classical philosophy, the assumption that there must be an essence in order to have something exist had been uncontested. Plato's *Theory of Forms* most certainly comes to mind in this context, and it clearly makes sense that, for example, all tables in the world share the same essence (=form). This concept works indeed well with the objects of the outer world; the objects have a clear and well defined meaning. According to Sartre such a conceptualization cannot apply to human life. There is no meaning per se in human life, a circumstance probably most of us experienced in our lifetimes. The experience of meaninglessness demonstrates the lack of essence. It appears that this meaninglessness of human life leads to the human desire of completion, what Sartre would name *ens causa sui*. "The self is individual; it is the individual completion of the self which haunts the for-itself" (Sartre, Being and Nothingness 141). The attempt to justify our existence, through trying to become the causation of ourselves,[1] has no prospect of success and thus human existence becomes a "useless passion" (Ibid 784). In religious life, God would provide the *ens causa sui*. However, for Sartre, there exists no God who would provide the human being as such with essence and he explains that

> [...] a creation ex nihilo can not explain the coming to pass of being; for if being is conceived in a subjectivity, even a divine subjectivity, it remains a mode of intra-subjective being. Such subjectivity can not have even the *representation* of an objectivity, and consequently it can not even be affected with the *will* to create the objective. (Sartre, Being and Nothingness 26)

If there were a God, he would consequently be separate from us. There is no one who can tell us what is wrong or right, no one who sets goals for us or who defines who we are. Since the human mind is not

---

[1] In the original Sartre writes: "Generally speaking there is no irreducible taste or inclination. They all represent a certain appropriative choice of being. It is up to existential psychoanalysis to compare and classify them. Ontology abandons us here; it has merely enabled us to determine the ultimate ends of human reality, its fundamental possibilities, and the value which haunts it. Each human reality is at the same time a direct project to metamorphose its own For-itself into an In-itself-For-itself and a project of the appropriation of the world as a totality of being-in-itself, in the form of a fundamental quality. Every human reality is a passion in that it projects losing itself so as to found being and by the same stroke to constitute the In-itself which escapes contingency by being its own foundation, the *Ens causa sui*, which religions call God. Thus the passion of man is the reverse of that of Christ, for man loses himself as man in order that God may be born. But the idea of God is contradictory and we lose ourselves in vain. Man is a useless passion." (Sartre, Being and Nothingness, 784)

only capable of negating, but also capable of conceptualizing possibilities, it is the human being himself, who must give meaning to his life. Or as Sartre puts it: "man first of all exists, encounters himself, surges up in the world and defines himself afterwards" (Sartre, Existentialism and Humanism 28).

According to Sartre human existence thus "is what it is not and is not what it is" (Sartre, Being and Nothingness 113), alluding to the inherent contradiction of human life as such, which results out of the interplay between *in-itself* and *for-itself*. The transcending *being-for-itself* subsequently implies a conceptualization of the self in the future. Consciousness is thus set by Sartre as "*being such that in its being, its being is in question in so far as this being implies a being other than itself*" (Ibid 24).

Following this logic, man is not only constituted by his facticity – meaning the "features of our 'situation' [...] given to us [that ...] are fixed from without" (Solomon, Introduction 36). Rather, the human condition implies that consciousness needs to negotiate past and future in order to establish the present in order to define ourselves (Macann 134). The past thus equals facticity, making a person's past *in-itself* (Sartre, Being and Nothingness 173). The conscious *being-for-itself*, conceptualizes the future and will have to take responsibility for its actions, as there are no god-given ethics:

> Man makes himself; he is not found ready-made: he makes himself by the choice of his morality, and he cannot but choose a morality, such is the pressure of circumstances upon him. We define man only in relation to his commitments; it is therefore absurd to reproach us for irresponsibility in our choice. (Sartre, Basic Writings 42)

Man thus is free; he is condemned to freedom. However, Sarte does not maintain that we are absolutely free, as there are limitations to our freedom. These limitations arise out of anguish that is created by the dichotomy of human existence. Nothingness allows us to be free in our consciousness, while our being in the world demands from us to make choices at the same time. Moreover,

11

Essence is all that human reality apprehends in itself as having been. It is here that anguish appears as an apprehension of self inasmuch as it exists in the perpetual mode of detachment from what is; better yet, in so far as it makes itself exist as such. For we can never apprehend an *Erlebnis* as a living consequence of that *nature* which is ours. The overflow of our consciousness progressively constitutes that nature, but it remains always behind us and it dwells in us as the permanent object of our retrospective comprehension. It is in so far as this nature is a demand without being a recourse that it is apprehended in anguish.

In anguish freedom is anguished before itself inasmuch as it is instigated and bound by nothing. (Sartre, Being and Nothingness 72-73)

Thus, there are several ways to escape our own freedom, our responsibility. With the help of what Sartre calls *everyday morality*, we can avoid *ethical anguish* as our everyday lives receive reified meaning through values, demands and the world itself. The underlying phenomenon Sartre calls the *spirit of seriousness*, which "views man as an object and subordinates him to the world" (Sartre, Being and Nothingness 806). We thus do not have to create and justify our own values and are able to escape our freedom (Suhr 121; see Sartre, Being and Nothingness 76). Another very popular escape route from radical freedom certainly is determinism. Either we presuppose a human nature (as a psychological determinism) or we reify ourselves. The latter implies a shift to the in-itself, meaning that we will act as if we were dealing with the own self from a "little-god-perspective," the self becomes an object ruled by a god inside ourselves (Suhr 121).

An authentic person, however, will "make himself," although it is impossible to determine for the most part whether a situation is the result of facticity or of transcendence. "To be a person is to be in a position of never being able to *know* what is given and what one can produce, and this means there can be no answer for a living man to the question 'Who am I?'" (Solomon, Introduction 36). The moment, we accept an answer for this particular question, "would be to accept a characterization of oneself as a 'given,' to make oneself inauthentic or put oneself in bad faith" (Ibid).

Through this delicate mechanism, which construes the interplay between our own facticity and transcendence, we can again avoid responsibility for our being and fall into bad faith or self-deception (*mauvaise foi*). This can be easily achieved by 'living' our formal identity, meaning to define ourselves through social categories, such as a profession, class status or race. Instead of realizing that through negation Nothingness allows us to become whatever we desire (Sartre calls this momentum 'The Great Human Stream'), which of course depends on certain circumstances (facticity), we can hide from our human constitution. Instead of transcending ourselves to truly become human, we can fall into bad faith and consequently make ourselves an object in the eyes of others (Suhr, Jean-Paul Sartre 125). Sartre provides us with a waiter as a typical example for somebody who has fallen into bad faith:

> 'Let us consider this waiter in the café. His movement is quick and forward, a little too precise, a little too rapid. He comes toward the customers with a step a little too quick. He bends forward a little too eagerly; his voice, his eyes express an interest a little too solicitous for the order of the client. Finally there he returns, trying to imitate in his walk the inflexible stiffness of some kind of automaton while carrying his tray with the recklessness of a tightrope-walker by putting it in a perpetually unstable, perpetually broken equilibrium which he perpetually re-establishes by a light movement of the arm and hand. All his behavior seems to us a game. He applies himself to linking his movements as though they were mechanisms, the one regulating the other; his gestures and even his voice seem to be mechanisms; he gives himself the quickness and pitiless rapidity of things. He is playing, he is amusing himself. But what is he playing? We need not watch long before we can explain it: he is playing at being a waiter in a café. (Sartre, Being and Nothingness 101-102)

The waiter's behavior must be seen as bad faith insofar, as he wants to become the idea of the waiter; an object just like a glass is a glass. Since, however, the waiter is human and has to "think" the ideal waiter, he separates himself from the object, which is the idea of the waiter. Yet, it is clear that in order to live in human society, we must necessarily take on particular roles at times. However, if we play the role to a point, where we convince ourselves and others that the role and the self are identical, we must speak of self-deception. In choosing to define our self as a thing, a role – the desperate endeavor to become *in-itself* – we evade taking responsibility to have to assign meaning to values and the world per se (Suhr 126-127). Sartre concludes that our anguish to be truly be human is anchored in our consciousness and bad faith is a simple consequence. However, through rejecting the *spirit of seriousness*, we could go through a "radical conversion of my being-in-the-world" (Sartre, Being and Nothingness 598), which Sartre unfortunately does not elaborate any further.

Another important part of Sartre's philosophy is *being-for-others*, which also limits our freedom through the reception of ourselves by others. However, we need others in order to gain knowledge about ourselves, since our realities are dependent on the interplay between the *being-for-itself* and the *being-for-others*, what Sartre calls "being-in-a-pair-with-the-other." Sartre uses the example of shame in order to illustrate the interdependency of the *for-itself* and the *for-others*. First, we are ashamed of what we are. Second, we are ashamed for what we represent for the other. Third, we accept the verdict of the other about us as what we are; we are what the other sees in us. And fourth, the other defines a new type of being for us, which is different from the *for-itself* – the *being for others*[2] (Suhr 136).

A very graphic allegory of the eavesdropper clarifies *being-for-others*:

> Let us imagine that moved by jealousy, curiosity, or vice I just glued my ear to the door and looked through a keyhole. I am alone and on the level of a non-thetic self-consciousness. This means first of all that there is no self to inhabit my consciousness, nothing therefore to which I can refer my acts in order to qualify

---

[2] In fact, *being-for-others* is located between *being-in-itself* and *being-for-itself*, as the other is not our own being, of which he has knowledge, while we who are our own being do not have knowledge about it (see Suhr, 150).

14

them. They are in no way *known*; I *am my acts* and hence they carry in themselves their whole justification. I am a pure consciousness *of* things,[3] and things, caught up in the circuit of my selfness, offer to me their potentialities as the proof of my non-thetic consciousness (of) my own possibilities. This means that behind that door a spectacle is presented as "to be seen," a conversation as "to be heard." The door, the keyhole are at once both instruments and obstacles; they are presented as "to be handled with care", the keyhole is given as "to be looked through close by and little to one side." (Sartre, Being and Nothingness 347-348)

The moment, however the eavesdropper is caught in the act of peeking through a keyhole, he "falls into the world," meaning that it is the gaze of another, which will stigmatize him (McBride 72). The pre-reflective act, inspired by jealousy and thus having been a free choice, becomes aware (Suhr 141-142). "It means that I am suddenly affected in my being and that essential modifications appear in my structure—modifications which I can apprehend and fix conceptually by means of the reflective *cogito*" (Sartre, Being and Nothingness 349). For the eavesdropper's self, the act is nothing but mere consciousness. For the other, however, the eavesdropper has become an object. This is why Sartre writes:

> My original fall is the existence of the Other. Shame—like pride—is the apprehension of myself as a nature although that very nature escapes me and is unknowable as such. Strictly speaking, it is not that I perceive myself losing my freedom in order to become a *thing*, but my nature is—over there, outside my lived freedom—as a given attribute of this being which I am for the Other. (Sartre, Being and Nothingness 352)

The other is subsequently the death of our own possibilities in regard to our transcendence; we thus fear the other. However, the other is necessary in order to see who we are. Yet here lies the danger of falling into bad faith once again, insofar as we might start to accept and define ourselves according to our perception by others.[4]

---

[3] Sartre speaks in this context of "pre-reflective" consciousness, which concerns itself with the outer world. This contrasts with the *being-for-itself*, which is a conscious act.

Particularly interesting, when referring to the subject of this analysis, are the roles of friendship, love and sexuality in the light of *being-for-others*. Since we always depend on how others view us, we want to win their affection in order to reaffirm our identities, ourselves. It follows that friendship and love can thus be seen as struggles for authenticity. According to Sartrean thought, friends are not chosen because we particularly like them, but because they reaffirm our conceptions about ourselves. The other has knowledge about what we are. "The other holds a secret—the secret of what I am. He makes me be and thereby he possesses me, and this possession in nothing other than the consciousness of possessing me" (Sartre, Being and Nothingness 475). Thus we are constantly trying to become the masters within a relationship, or to free ourselves from "mental slavery." Since "being-as-object is an unbearable contingency, [...] I have to recover my freedom [...] in order to be the foundation of myself. But this is conceivable only if I assimilate the Other's freedom. Thus my project of recovering myself is fundamentally a project of absorbing the Other" (Sartre, Being and Nothingness 475). Human relationships accordingly develop into mechanisms of sadism or masochism when loves and friendships fail. Sadism arises when we fail in winning the other over, masochism chooses submission as a strategy to force the other to please us.

---

[4] Remember in this context Heidegger's *Das Man self*.

2.2. An Outline of Albert Camus' Philosophy

Never accepting himself labeled as a philosopher, but seeing himself as a writer, Albert Camus (1913-1960) concerns himself with the experience of the absurd. Absurdity as a human experience establishes itself in the irreconcilable gap between the self and the world; we feel alienated whenever we look behind the scenes of daily routines and encounter the world's animosity. "A step lower and strangeness creeps in: perceiving that the world is 'dense,' sensing to what degree a stone is foreign and irreducible to us, with what intensity nature or a landscape can negate us" (Camus 12). It is our desire for harmony, unity and meaning that consequently puts us into a state of despair in the face of a "world [that] evades us" (Ibid). "The absurd is born of this confrontation between the human need and the unreasonable silence of the world" (Ibid 26). It is in this context that Camus writes "There is but one truly serious philosophical problem and that is suicide" (Ibid 1). The suicide that Camus is addressing here, is the one that is never being committed, although it would be the logical consequence in the light of the evidence about human existence as such (Brée 219).

We thus have to relinquish the quest for any metaphysical interpretation of our lives; there is none to be found. It follows that the absurd has to be our sole certainty and to give up any hopes for the ulterior. Rather, we should take the world as it is as a given and live up to our humanity: "I come at last to death and to the attitude we have towards it. [...] Properly speaking, nothing has been experienced but what has been lived and made conscious" (Camus 13-14). It is the human fate to accept suffering, while living in a world without meaning and without a god.

Camus famously compares the human existence with the Greek myth of Sisyphus. It is he, who is the hero of the absurd, the ultimate allegory of the *condition humaine*. Being condemned by the gods to the never ending task of rolling a rock up a mountain, which would fall back of its own weight, only to having to repeat this scene all over again, is probably the most futile task imaginable. However, Sisyphus is conscious about himself and about his situation and thus cannot deny the absurd state he finds himself in. Instead of giving up, Sisyphus holds on to his dignity by "throwing himself into this task and thus into his life" (Arrington 185). It is the conscious act of performing a futile task in a meaningless world that saves Sisyphus from despair: "At each of those moments when he leaves the heights and gradually sinks toward the lairs of the gods, he is superior to his fate" (Camus 117). Camus further explains:

> Sisyphus, proletarian of the gods, powerless and rebellious, knows the whole extent of his wretched condition: it is what he thinks of during his descent. The lucidity that was to constitute his torture at the same time crowns his victory. There is not fate that cannot be surmounted by scorn. (Ibid)

Although distracted by our everyday lives, the absurd will eventually jump at us in many a form. A feeling of time trickling off, captures our attention, leading to our revolt against our mortality (Brée 220). "We live on the future: 'tomorrow', 'later on', 'when you have made your way', 'you will understand when you are old enough'. Such irrelevancies are wonderful, for, after all, it's a matter of dying. Yet a time comes when a man notices or says that he is thirty. Thus he asserts his youth" (Camus 12). The absurd also comes along in the strangeness of the outer world—as already noted before— and in humanity itself.

> Men, too, secrete the inhuman. At certain moments of lucidity, the mechanical aspect of their gestures, their meaningless pantomime make silly everything that surrounds them. A man is talking on the telephone behind a glass partition; you cannot hear him but you see his incomprehensible dumb-show: you wonder why he is alive. The discomfort in the face of man's own inhumanity, this incalculable tumble before the image of what we are, this 'nausea', as a writer of today calls it, is also the absurd. Likewise the stranger who at certain seconds comes to meet us in a mirror, the familiar and yet alarming brother we encounter in our own photographs is also the absurd. (Camus 13)

In this absurdity, however, we have to return to the question of suicide. Does it make sense? Camus' answer is clear: It makes less sense than living in the face of the revolt against the absurd. "It may be thought that suicide follows revolt—but wrongly. For it does not represent the logical outcome of revolt. It is just the contrary by the consent it presupposes. [...] His future, his unique and dreadful future—he sees and rushes toward it. In its way, suicide settles the absurd" (Camus 52). The revolt against death, becomes the only possible mindset for us. Now, man can become the absurd man, a man who does not yearn. Instead of resolving life's absurdity with suicide, death becomes his enemy and he commits himself to life. It is the refusal of his own meaninglessness that will shape the absurd man. For the sake of his own identity, man must hold onto the demand for unity and meaning (Brée 222-223).

In his essay *The Rebel*, Camus advances the idea of absurdity further. As we are not alone in facing absurdity, the absurd consciousness will let the individual recognize "the communality of our condition" (Sagi 108). Solidarity thus becomes the basis of any revolt as the individual identifies with others who suffer. Using *Prometheus*[5] as an allegory, Camus points at the possibility of sacrificing oneself for a greater good, such as freedom or justice.[6] For the purpose of the analysis at hand, it is ample though to note that there is an existentialist notion of solidarity in facing an absurd world.

More than interesting in the context of the subject of this analysis, is Camus' take on love and sexuality, for which he uses Don Juan as an allegory.

> If it were sufficient to love, things would be too easy. The more one loves the stronger the absurd grows. It is not through lack of love that Don Juan goes from woman to woman. It is ridiculous to represent him as a mystic in quest of total love. But it is indeed because he loves them with the same passion and each time with his

---

[5] Who, in Greek mythology, stole knowledge from Zeus in order to share it with the suffering mortals.
[6] Camus also explains the role of revolts gone wrong, such as fascism, but this is irrelevant at this instance.

whole self that he must repeat his gift and his profound quest. (Camus 67)

It is Don Juan's passion for human diversity that drives him, and weariness will never befall him, as he does it with all his heart (Brée 224). He fulfills Sartre's claim not to hope for the otherworldly, but to "exploit" life as much as possible, as it is all we have.[7]

---

[7] Two other absurd heroes are introduced in *The Myth of Sisyphus*, the actor and the conqueror, but they are omitted in this narrative, since they are extraneous to the subject of this analysis.

2.3. Towards the Existentialist Hero

At this point, it makes sense to define how existentialist heroism manifests itself. Clearly, an existentialist hero's characterization will evolve around issues of consciousness, freedom, choice, morality, and his way of dealing with the outer world and other people.

The key idea of existentialism, that existence precedes essence, will primarily require an existentialist hero to recognize the chaotic, unstructured, and random nature of human life. For the hero, we are looking for in this analysis, the world presents itself as an absurd place, where one is being thrown into life, having little control over what is happening and lacking insight into the mechanisms of the world at large. Although our hero has no other option than to realize his absurd life, he cannot resign to absurdity, as "our only salvation lies in not becoming resigned" (Murdoch, Existentialist Hero 115). It is the Camusean rebellion against the absurd world, that ultimately is able to provide us with some meaning in life. An existentialist hero thus faces the meaninglessness of death, does not despair, and eventually creates meaning in the face of absurdity. Accordingly, we can imagine the existentialist hero as "an anxious man trying to impose or assert or find himself" (Murdoch, Existentialists 227). The momentum in which an existentialist hero defines meaning, can thus be seen as the being-for-itself's longing for meaning in nothingness; or at least to remedy this consciousness of emptiness with something other than emptiness itself.

Obviously there is the danger for such a person to turn into an egoist as this "hero is the new version of the romantic man, the man of power, abandoned by God, struggling on bravely, sincerely and alone. This image consoles by showing us man as strong, self-reliant and uncrushable" (Ibid). However, a revolt against absurdity cannot be a solemn endeavor as it would fail, as egoism would just add up to the traits of the absurd world. In order to be able to create meaning in an otherwise meaningless world, the existentialist hero must acknowledge that others have to face absurdity just like himself. In this context, the existentialist hero will reach out to others and act in ways of solidarity, which has enormous implications for the hero's ethical understanding.

Logically, the insight that our existence in this hostile world amounts to absurdity, will lead the existentialist hero to experiment with life. In doing so, the person in question will subsequently reject "god-given" values and go out into the world and define his own set of values. It is a common misconception that existentialism would reject the idea of values as an integral part of life. In fact, existentialism comes quite close to establishing its own ethics, when considering that it is often "hinted that, when placing our own values and meanings, certain moves are preferable to certain others" (Murdoch, Existentialist Hero 110). The existentialist hero will define his existence through being-for-itself, not only allowing him to overcome the past (the being-in-itself), but also allowing for change in his value system.

It appears in this light that an existentialist hero will reject everyday morality—as it appears to be doctrinaire—to a very high degree and live according to his individual moral system that results from experience. Thus the existentialist establishment of values is arrived at in the context of a presupposed freedom from a behaviorist light: "The moral agent is free to withdraw, survey the facts, and choose again" (Murdoch, Vision and Choice 83). Consequently, existentialist heroes are open to modification in regard to their individual values—they will adjust their morality when life interferes with obsolete or impedimentary values. This is, however, not to equate with "moral flexibility," as our existential heroes would not alter their ways out of opportunistic motives, but upon the realization of their misconceptions regarding certain circumstances. An existentialist hero's moral code will evolve out of the insight that each person is a free being, surrounded by other free beings (Murdoch, Existentialist Hero 110) and he must face the question of how he is supposed to conduct himself amongst these other free beings in an absurd world. Clearly, freedom lies at the base of an existentialist value system, as an existentialist hero will create such a system "with lucid consciousness of his responsibility, reaffirming his values, while knowing that they depend only on him" (Ibid 122). It is in fact the ability to doubt once established meanings and values that marks an existentialist hero in action (Ibid 124). It is exactly this doubt, which will save our hero from falling into doctrinaire values; we shall be reminded that authoritarianism was able to facilitate even humanistic values for ideological purposes (cf. Zima 37).

In such a light it becomes clear, that each individual and existentialist being must construct his own set of values. Murdoch (Vision and Choice 82) argues:

> [...] moral differences look less like differences of choice, given the same facts, and more like differences of vision. In other words, a moral concept seems less like a moveable and extensible ring laid down to cover a certain area of fact, and more like a total difference of *Gestalt*. We differ not only because we select different objects out of the same world but because we see different worlds [...]

Moreover, a hero of the absurd who is confronted with an indifferent world, must come to the conclusion that meaning cannot be found in societal values, as they create an illusion of meaning. True meaning can thus only be found outside the moral limitations of society (Zima 144-145), defined in revolt against one's absurd existence. However, and this is a crucial point in existentialism: excuses are not an option. As we are free to chose our actions and values, everything we do and everything we do not (!) do is on our watch.

Values are closely related to an authentic life. In this context, Sartre's idea of bad faith moves into the scene. Since an existentialist hero will never accept outside values (everyday morality), he also must reject to being ascribed a role. Instead of becoming a simplified "something" for others, our hero will define himself and not become the emblematic Sartrean waiter. In order to avoid bad faith, the existentialist hero must refuse ideas about class, race or ideology—particularly when others try to impose such categories on him. Simultaneously thus, the existentialist hero will transcend his being-for-others if it is connoted in a negative way. Moreover, in challenging his being-for-others, our existentialist hero will be able to prevent becoming an object. Instead of becoming being-in-it, our hero will struggle for his identity being reflected as being-for-it in order to remain authentic (Ibid 39).

One area in which existential emptiness can be temporarily filled is sexuality. The existential hero has to be aware of his sexual desires and the ways in which he deals with them. From a Camusean perspective our hero has to indulge in his sexuality and live it to the fullest, not caring for societal restrictions. However, when sexuality and love are apparent at the same time—including infidelity—an existential hero has to be aware that his actions are to be seen in the context of the sadism and masochism.

As will be shown in parts two and three of this analysis, Irving's characters fulfill the existentialist criteria proposed by Camus and Sartre.

3. John Irving's Novels and Existentialism

3.1. The Water-Method Man

The novel in question starts off with Fred "Bogus" Trumper paying a visit to a urologist, whom his girlfriend Tulpen had recommended to him. The visit's purpose is to help find a cure for Trumper's long term ailment—a birth defect in his urinary tract that transforms it into a "narrow winding road." The defect in question prevents common bacteria to be flushed out easily after intercourse, as would be the case with "*normal* penises," essentially causing him pain during emiction and sexual climax. Dr. Jean-Claude Vigneron has four solutions available for Trumper: drugs, abstaining from sexual intercourse, surgery or the water-method.[8] Needless to say, Trumper chooses the water method, for he is not a "practical, no-nonsense sort of man."

At that time Trumper has recently left his former life in Iowa behind. There he was married to Sue "Biggie" Kunft—a former member of the United States Olympic ski team, whom he met during a skiing trip to Kaprun while Trumper was studying German at Vienna University. The two of them have a son, Colm. In Iowa, Trumper—always short on funds—had been working on his PhD thesis at the University of Iowa; a translation of the Old Low Norse poem *Akthelt and Gunnel*. In the process 'Bogus' Trumper made up whole passages, which "made the translation of *Akthelt and Gunnel* easier [as] it's very hard to tell real Old Low Norse from made-up Old Low Norse" (Water-Method Man 31). At the time of his visit to the urologist, Trumper is living with Tulpen in New York City, where he works as a sound engineer for independent filmmaker Ralph Packer—one of Trumper's childhood friends—whose avant-garde films revolve around personal conflicts and social issues. To make things more complicated, Tulpen had been briefly romantically

---

[8] Clearing the urinary tract after intercourse through urination, requiring the consumption of huge amounts of water before sexual engagement.

involved with Ralph Packer. It is he who intends to turn "Trumper's own tangled and irresolute existence" (Harter and Thompson 41) into a movie called *Fucking Up*—the title being emblematic for the course of Trumper's life.

Trumper is about to "fuck things" up yet once again, when Tulpen—whom Trumper feels somewhat uncomfortable with—wants to have a baby. In spite of his refusing to commit himself to a new family, by referring to his son Colm as being "enough," Tulpen still gets pregnant and thus Trumper switches into escapism. He travels to Vienna in order to find his friend Merrill Overturf, whose "winsomely reckless conduct is a constant temptation away from the duties of Iowa [and] the lessons of New York" (Klinkowitz 47).

Not only learning that Merrill Overturf died two years ago in a senseless accident—while trying to impress an American girl, Trumper also learns Overturf drowned in the Danube in an endeavor to find a mysterious World War II tank. During this visit to Vienna Trumper also gets himself involved in the drug-trafficking business and suffers a nervous breakdown. His stay in Vienna ends when narcotics agents provide him with a ticket to the United States and a limo ride from JFK airport into New York City, after he had turned informant. However, as it is, Trumper, instead of returning to New York City, talks the limo driver into driving him to Maine, where he wants to find his childhood friend Cuthbert "Couth" Bennett, who supported Trumper when he was in financial need in Iowa. When Trumper arrives at the Pillsbury estate—of which Couth is the caretaker—he not only encounters Couth but finds that Biggie, Colm and Couth are about to become a family. After that life altering situation, Trumper returns once more to New York City.

The incident at the Pillsbury estate triggers a process of change in Trumper who suddenly has to realize that he has never been able to finish anything in his life—his endings avoidance, as Klinkowitz (45) sees it. In an attempt to finish something, Trumper returns to Iowa in order to complete his dissertation on *Akthelt and Gunnel*. There he lives in the basement of his dissertation advisor's home, this time producing a proper translation and finally being awarded his PhD degree.

However, Trumper's tying up of "loose ends" (Campbell 38) in his life has just begun. Subsequently, Trumper reconciles with his father, who during his first period in Iowa had cancelled financial support for Trumper. Additionally he finally has surgery on his urinary tract. In the meantime Tulpen has given birth to their son Merrill, whom she named after Trumper's much admired friend Merrill Overturf, and she accepts Trumper back into her life. Having been awarded his PhD, Trumper is about to attain a teaching position, and Packer's movie *Fucking Up* not only receives outstanding reviews, but also makes Trumper sort of a celebrity.

In the end, *The Water-Method Man* turns into a "celebration of the flesh, marriage, fertility, and family" (Ibid), which manifests itself in a coming together of three families at the Pillsbury estate in celebrating Throgshafen day: Ralph Packer's fiancé Matje is pregnant, Biggie and Couth are finally married and have a child together and Trumper has managed to maintain a stable relationship with Tulpen.

In *The Water-Method Man*, we thus encounter a protagonist, whose existence could be best described by referring to him as someone having an air of chaos surrounding him and as someone who is "wrecked with self-doubts" (Priestly, Structure 22), but who nevertheless remains a simpatico character. Always remaining indecisive—which first becomes apparent in his early wrestling career in which he never finished a match—Trumper's problem involving indecision revolves around flight. Trumper's affinity for 'incompleteness'—his avoiding endings, as already mentioned—found its way into the novel's title. Born with a birth defect that turned his urinary tract into "a narrow winding road" meant he would have to undergo surgery in order to prevent infections, a step he postponed taking for a good part of his life.

Trumper's character is contrasted with Tulpen, "a young woman whose maturity and self-control [help] to compensate for [Trumper's] own lack of these qualities" (Harter and Thompson 41). Trumper's lacking these character traits seems to stem from his "mush-minded ability to read his own sentimentality into everything around him" (Water-Method Man 33). Not coincidentally did Irving choose to describe Trumper's urinary tract as a "narrow winding road," for it can be seen as a metaphor for "the evasions and repressions" (Shostak, Family Romances 88) in Trumper's life. His vulnerability becomes apparent when he suspends his PhD thesis by stopping "translating with Stanza 280 because the doom of Akthelt and Gunnel seemed inevitable: 'The world was too strong'—for them and for Trumper" (Priestly, Structure 22). Trumper's sympathy for the vulnerable becomes apparent in his former wife Biggie's struggle against a mouse living in the basement. Klinkowitz notes: "[…] Fred Trumper identifies with the underdog and sees his own perilous condition as similar to that of the mouse Biggie is trying to trap in the basement. Each night Trumper sneaks down the stairs to spring the mousetrap" (46).

It appears that Trumper defines his own sense of the world and his overall morality out of a certain sensitivity towards the world's cruelty. However, there remains the question how Trumper would constantly end up in uncomfortable situations until he begins to change. It seems that rather than being "a man making himself," Trumper's handling of life fluctuates between embracing everyday morality, his awareness of human existence in absurdity and a misconception of freedom. From an existentialist perspective, for instance, Trumper's marriage to the pregnant Biggie—whom he has long not been in love with anymore—could be seen as a lapse into everyday morality and thus a flight from moral freedom. This becomes particularly clear during his failed attempt to have sex in the cornfields with Lydia Kindle, an Iowa undergrad student, where he finds himself unable to perform and which "leads to double exposure: of his 'prick' and of himself as a 'prick'" (Campbell 36). What Irving does at this juncture is clearly a comic riff, but in the context of the existentialist notion of everyday morality also revealing: clearly, at this point Trumper is governed by a morality that is not his own: "His characterization of the scene [with Lydia] dissuades him: all he can think of is her avenging family" (Davis and Womack 51). One might argue at this point that his everyday morality is rooted in his upbringing. Thus, for example, when "Trumper is fifteen, he and Couth get the "clap" from Elsbeth Malkas, a local girl; Dr. Trumper [Bogus' father and a physician] responds with puritanical rage and penicillin" (Campbell 45). Besides this Sartrean example of everyday morality, there is also a clear reference within this scene to the world's cruelty, which makes the incident with Lydia Kindle even more interesting, as "once he begins to undress her the childlike underthings she wears remind him of vulnerable little Colm" (Davis and Womack 51). It is the realization of Lydia Kindle's vulnerability in this scene that adds to Trumper's lapse into the everyday moralist's expectation of repercussion for one's immoral deeds:

> [...] her long fingers point down, unmoving, and the cloudy sun through the window is just strong enough to glint off her high school ring; it is too big for her finger and has slipped askew.
> I shut my eyes in her powdered cleavage, noting a sort of candy musk. But why does my mind run to slaughterhouses, and to all the young girls raped in wars? (Water-Method Man 179)

Nonetheless, Trumper, instead of leaving an unhappy marriage, puts himself into a situation, for which in the world of *Akhelt and Gunnel* he would be "deballed with a battle ax" (Reilly 43).

If this were a psychoanalytic analysis,[9] it might be tempting to argue that Trumper forgetting to remove the condom from the unsuccessful seduction adventure, can actually be seen in a Freudian context. Particularly, since Trumper was not conscious of still wearing the condom.

> Then I had my fly open, and my feet painfully spread to straddle the hopper. I fumbled myself out and commenced to pee, while Biggie stared grimly at my pecker and watched me fill up the condom. Until the pressure and lack of noise was suddenly, awfully apparent to me, and I gazed down to see my growing balloon. (Water-Method Man 191)

---

[9] It might be argued that psychoanalysis and existentialism are more related than commonly acknowledged.

It thus would certainly be possible to argue, that his being exposed as the adulterous husband, allows him to move away from a desolate marriage. On another note, however, this scene can be read as truly existentialist in the context of being-for-others. Trumper himself, does not consider himself as cheating on his wife in the events around his encounter with Lydia Kindle. It is rather Biggie who "misreads the essential of Trumper's oddball situation" (Klinkowitz 52) and who ultimately labels him an adulterer. Yet, this is the second time Trumper got into trouble for having been misread: Some time ago, he had been exposed as an adulterer, when Lydia Kindle had provided him comfort and left lipstick on his cheek after an unfortunate event where Trumper worked as a part-time salesman at an Iowa football game, and his sales board got destroyed. Klinkowitz thus detects "a common Trumper routine: self discovery, from which one would think he'd learn a collective lesson, but then the mistaken discovery by Biggie, who gets the facts all wrong and sets Trumper off again down the slapstick course of his long and winding road" (49). Yet, "the only self-knowledge gained from all this is Trumper's determination that in any place or circumstance he'd never succeed" (Ibid 50). In such a manner of depicting Trumper's "fall into the world," *The Water-Method Man*, thus comprises another element of Sartrean philosophy in perfecting the interplay between being-for-itself and being-for-others. It is Biggie's *gaze* that judges him and defines him, making him pay "for his impulse toward infidelity" (Miller, Irving 57).

Yet, feeling guilt, when imposing pain to people one is close to, can also be seen as a trait of existentialist solidarity. In this context, the role of Trumper most certainly is an ambiguous one. On the one had, he hurts the women around him by leaving or not committing himself to them. On the other hand, Trumper cares about people—he even cares about mice. Thus in *The Water-Method Man*, "[adorable] children appear who must be protected from the world's cruelty" (Epstein 43), and to the little mouse in the basement Trumper whispers: "Don't be frightened. I'm on *your* side" (Water-Method Man 68).

In the context of Trumper's unstable relationships with women, Campbell provides us with an interesting interpretation, which on the one hand goes beyond existentialism as such, but on the other hand alludes to ideas about freedom and self-definition.

> No wonder he is afraid of Sue "Biggie" Kunft, whose coming (*Zu-kunft*) threatens to dominate his life. When he sees her cleaning their house, he gapes at her "as if she were some animal, ugly and scary and able to eat me whole." This image of the devouring (castrating) mother, with her "breasts flopping," is both ugly and horrific. Trumper exhibits similar fears of castration with Tulpen. In her apartment, the bed is surrounded by fish tanks, in which fish face the prospect of being eaten or drowning in the murky water; for Trumper, being with Tulpen is also like drowning. (Campbell 49)

From such a perspective it becomes rather clear, why Trumper is having difficulty in maintaining stable love-relationships with women. Moreover, though not to a Camusean extent, Trumper can also be seen as a Don Juanesque character, since although he would not actually complete the adulterous act, he still "lusts after [Lydia Kindle]" (Miller, Irving 56).

Returning to questions of human solidarity in an absurd, and in the context of Irving's work, violent world, Trumper's concern for children and all living creatures is certainly one of his most outstanding character traits. This becomes apparent in his relationship to his son, in the episode in which he chose to drive Colm back to Maine, instead of "risking" his son's live aboard an airplane (Water-Method Man 202). Also, he would check at night to see if Colm still were breathing, or hide behind the bushes and follow when "Colm rides his tricycle around the block" (Reilly 41). Actually, his concern for others extends beyond his family and children. We learn, for example, that he rescues a "faggot" in a bar.

31

Clearly, Camus' notion of the world's animosity and human solidarity as a consequence comes to mind. As Miller notes:

> The overpowering pressure of external reality is central to Irving's fiction, and the sense of it traumatizes his protagonists, especially such sensitive ones as Trumper [and Garp], who react to the world by trying to withdraw from it, desperately attempting to shelter their children from any exposure to pain or suffering. (Irving 53-54)

Yet, this sense of human vulnerability juxtaposed with the "overpowering pressure of external reality" leads to the truly existentialist question Trumper poses: "How is everything related to anything else?" Beyond the plot, the novel presents itself exactly as "a kind of puzzle" (Miller, Irving 50) which evolves around this question. Trumper subsequently can be described as "an absolute paranoiac victimized by his own self-analysis" (Water-Method Man 359), words a reviewer of the movie *Fucking Up* used to describe him. Throughout the novel, the neurotic Trumper is juxtaposed with his girlfriend Tulpen, "who has outgrown having to talk about herself" (Water-Method Man 18).

Another viable route to understanding Trumper's character development through an existentialist lens is to approach his escapism from the perspective of his stance on freedom; or better; how he manages a transition from an irresponsible, undetermined understanding of freedom toward a form of freedom in which he is able to commit himself, one in which he finally "makes himself." In order to do this, we have to look once again at one of his infamous escapes. When living in New York City, Fred Trumper notoriously flees from his self-contained world, using the movie and an imagined infidelity with Ralph Packer on Tulpen's part, while he had been hospitalized for urinary surgery, as excuses. Presenting the need to complete his suspended PhD thesis at Iowa University as his reason to leave New York City and to start a "new life," Trumper in reality is fleeing Tulpen's decision to have a baby and—due to her "losing" her intrauterine device—her actual pregnancy. What follows is a trip to

Austria in order to find his friend Merrill Overturf, who we already noted above had been dead for two years. In this context Harter and Thompson conclude that Trumper "continues to suffer from a long-time ailment: entrenched immaturity and the accompanying inability to accept responsibility" (41-42).

Ideas about freedom can be found throughout the novel and can be analyzed through an existentialist lens. It seems that Trumper's ambiguous relationship with freedom is one of the keys in understanding the novel from an existentialist perspective. On the one hand, Trumper cannot help himself but to be free—which coincides with his many escapes, which we encounter throughout the novel—while on the other hand having to realize that the "Merrill Overturfish" freedom he admires in his own times of despair, is probably not the one he really wants for himself. Although it is in the end exactly a quarrel with Biggie about Merrill that puts an end to his marriage, "he [Trumper] must come, if only subconsciously, to recognize that Merrill's kind of freedom was a form of cowardice or—at best—selfishness" (Ibid 49). Merrill's "cowardice" can be best understood if putting Camus' thought into context, which claims that rebellion against an absurd life can only take place in the context of solidarity; yet it becomes clear during the momentous skiing trip to Kaprun that there is no space for solidarity in Merrill Overturf's life:

> "You're not any fun to be with," Merrill told me. "You're in love, you know," he said. "And that's no fun at all . . ."
> "No, he's not in love," said Biggie. "We're not in love at all." She looked at me for reassurance, as if to say, We're not, are we?
> "Certainly not," I said, but I was nervous.
> "You certainly are," said Merrill, "you poor stupid bastard . . ." Biggie looked at him, shocked. "Jesus, you too," he told her. "You're both in love. I don't want anything to do with either of you."
> And he had sweet little to do with either of us, by God; we hardly ever saw him in Vienna. (Water-Method Man 138)

It appears that Trumper—as long as he worships Merrill Overturf like a hero—is a character who has not yet achieved "his" freedom, in the Sartrean sense. Only when he starts to realize that his strategy of running away has alienated him from his dear ones, is he able to redefine himself after suffering from a nervous breakdown. This process is triggered when Trumper finds himself in Vienna, looking for the late Merrill Overturf—"the great illusion" of his life—and "that part of Trumper that denies life and therefore cannot grow, must be killed off so that Trumper can finally transcend his own adolescent, escapist tendencies" (Harter and Thompson 49).

Upon returning to the United States, Trumper goes to see his childhood friend Couth in Maine, who is to Trumper's shock now living with Biggie and his son Colm. This instance can be seen as a turning point in Trumper's life as it "prompts [...] him to grow up" (Campbell 38). Returning to New York City, finally having been awarded a PhD degree and finding himself being a father again—in his absence, Tulpen gave birth to their son Merrill—Trumper faces a situation where he is confronted with the task of imposing "a viable structure" (Priestly, Structure 22) upon his life. Fred can finally transform from someone "who is coming apart at the seams, concerned only with saving himself" (Miller, Irving 48) into someone who acts responsible—particularly towards the people he cares about. The novel thus ends on a positive, happy note, where Trumper is able to finally accept Biggie being remarried to his best friend Couth, Tulpen's faithfulness and being a father. Harter and Thompson thus regard the plot as something like Trumper's "reentry into a life of responsibility and human commitment [and a] general reconciliation and a celebration of marriage and childbirth—in terms of the comic vision, of life itself" (42). In other words: "Irving tells the story of Fred 'Bogus' Trumper, who grows from an irresponsible bumbler, incapable of making decisions or commitments, to a man who settles down to work and family" (Campbell 35).

Sartrean thought can be found again in Trumper's dealing with facticity and transcendence and subsequently the relationship between the being-for-itself and being-for-others. Trumper, "can see his past quite objectively; it is the present he cannot deal with, for here are too many 'little things' weighing him down" (Miller, Irving 51). In other words, Trumper has no problem confronting his facticity—he is aware of it—however, in terms of the Sartrean for-itself, he constantly faces the existentialist trauma of self-definition. Also, the relationship of being-for-itself and being-in-itself (and subsequently facticity) can be found not only in the plot, but also in the novel's metastructure:

> The effect achieved is that of a continual refocusing of dual lenses, the first person clearly solipsistic and the third person more objective. This distinction is not destroyed by ultimately discovering what we early suspect, that both voices are actually Trumper's; whether obviously inside or only apparently outside his mind, we recognize that vantage point is crucial. This "autobiography" makes use of more than one device to create a sense of its author's consciousness; it provides a refraction of perspective that allows us to feel the tension between fact and feeling, experience and the impression it leaves. (Harter and Thompson 42-43)

Moreover, the constant change in perspective and the juxtaposition of his life periods "offer us simultaneously cause and effect; Trumper's funny-sad attempts at self-control and self-knowledge are located not in some vague, reported past, but always in the living present" (Ibid 43). Additionally, the novel's play with facticity and transcendence becomes apparent throughout the novel as Trumper gradually changes—something which fulfils the existentialist claim of "man making himself." Harter and Thompson note that "the interleafing of time" in the novel "is especially effective regarding the critical parallel between his relationships with Biggie and Tulpen; here we see both repetition and significant change, as does Trumper himself" (43). Clearly, Trumper can transcend from "the ways that people have of destroying each other (Miller, Good Wrestler 49)" towards sane relationships. If we view Trumper's relationship with

Biggie as failed—as a sadistic period in Trumper's life—his relationship with Tulpen certainly escaped this vicious circle.

The momentum of being-for-others is probably the most interesting twist in *Water-Method Man*, in the context of which Irving plays with Trumper's existentialist momentum of "who he really is." A quarrel with Tulpen reveals that 'Bogus' Trumper will remain "inaccessible [to others] until he has first become accessible to *himself*" (Harter and Thompson 46).

> "He says you don't come across, Trumper."
> "Come across?"
> "No one knows you, Trumper! You don't *convey* anything. You don't know much, either. Things just sort of happen to you, and they don't even add up to anything. You don't make anything of what happens to you. Ralph says you must be very complicated, Trumper. He thinks you must have a mysterious core under the surface."
> Trumper stared into the fish tank. *Where is the talking eel?*
> "And what do *you* think, Tulpen?" he asked her. "What do you think's under the surface?"
> "Another surface," she said, and he stared at her. "Or maybe just that one surface," she said, "with nothing under it.
> (Water-Method Man 93-94)

However, the novel creates a momentum of possible salvation through Trumper's "conscious unawareness of himself." In contrast to "other characters, who suffer from an excess of self-knowledge while yet unable to extricate themselves from the various traps in which they find themselves" (Miller, Irving 50), Trumper "quite naturally displays his creative tendencies as he gropes toward self-understanding" (Harter and Thompson, 44).

Learning, that the novel *is* Trumper's work,[10] it is not surprising that Harter and Thompson conclude that

> [it] is not simply that to "know thyself" remains the central injunction of Western culture—and is endlessly reiterated in the popular slogans of the counterculture in which Trumper lives—but that to know thyself by creating in its entirety one's reality in the only mode for the existential [!!!] writer to adopt. (45)

Trumper thus facilitates art as a means for resolving the existential crisis—"What was first a diary (life) in now a true story (art) [...] with Trumper finally underway toward a resolution" (Klinkowitz, 54-55). It is at this point that it makes sense to return to Trumper's being-for-others, as this "mode of existence" does not necessarily imply that the consequences of being gazed at must be solely negative, such as had been the case with Biggie who had "thrown Trumper into the world" as an adulterous man. Thus, the movie about Trumper, *Fucking Up*, can be regarded a tool which helps Trumper to finally grasp himself (his being-for-itself) through the lens of a camera (being-for-others). The movie turns out to have a "necessary therapeutic effect" (Ibid 54) as Trumper realizes that he should keep a diary in order to answer his question "How is anything related to anything else?" Here we are thrown back to chapter one, which in fact is the start of Trumper's diary.

3.2. The World According to Garp

The narrative of Irving's epic novel *The World According to Garp* starts during World War II. We encounter nurse Jenny Fields, who wants to have a child, but refuses the idea of sharing her offspring and her life with a man. Thus, while working at a hospital and encountering her soon-to-be-dead patient Technical Sergeant Garp,

---

[10] This becomes clear towards the end of the novel, where Trumper actually starts writing *The Water-Method Man*.

who suffers from brain damage, she becomes pregnant from him in a truly absurd way by having intercourse with him while he is unconscious. She names her son after his deceased father: T.S. Garp.

Garp grows up at Steering school, a New England boarding school, where his mother found a job as school nurse. Later on in the novel, Garp attends Steering school. His time at Steering is spent with the Percy children—whose mother is the heiress of the school estate. The Percy's dog bites off one of Garp's ears and he loses his virginity with one of the Percy daughters, Cushie. However, his devotion is dedicated to the wrestling teacher's daughter, Helen Holm. Helen, who is a passionate reader, one day announces that the only man she would ever marry, would be a "true" writer. Hence, Garp decides to become a "true" writer in order to win Helen's attention.

However, the route to becoming a writer is not an easy one, as Garp is still young and lacking life experience. Thus, after graduating from Steering School, Garp and his mother Jenny move to Vienna in order to provide Garp with the necessary stimulus. While Garp "absorbs experience" in excelling "mostly in lustful experiences" (Campbell 72) with Charlotte, a Viennese prostitute who is dying from cancer, Jenny is writing her soon-to-be-famous autobiography *A Sexual Suspect*. Upon Garp's and Jenny's return to the United States, Jenny—against her intentions and will—becomes the figure-head of the increasingly emerging feminist movement, as her autobiography is seen as a thorough feminist manifesto. In contrast to Jenny, it takes Garp a long while until he is able to write his first "real" short story *Pension Grillparzer*, which "convinces" Helen Holm to marry him.

After their marriage, Helen—who received her PhD in English literature at 23—teaches at a university, while Garp finds himself in the process of writing his first novel and being a devoted father to their first child Duncan. Upon the birth of their second son, Walt, the Garps encounter the Fletchers, with whom they start a love quadrangle. During this period, Garp is working on his second novel *The Second Wind of Cuckold*. Upon the end of the "partner exchange program" with the Fletcher's, Helen starts an affair with Michael Milton, one of her literature students. However, the relationship is revealed to Garp by

Milton's ex-girlfriend, who demands that Helen end the affair immediately. While she is "ending" things with Milton, Garp goes to the movies with Duncan and Walt, who has a cold. Due to the increasing severity of the cold, Garp and the boys return home earlier than expected. Garp's car crashes into Milton's car—who is receiving oral sex from Helen for the last time—leaving Walt dead, Duncan one eyed and Milton with a third of his former penis.

Of course, the Garps have to recover from this shock, and in order to do so, they retreat to Jenny's estate at Dog's Head Harbor, where she has established a healing haven for abused and victimized women. Upon Helen's and Garp's reconciliation, the family expects a new baby—Jenny, who is named after her grandmother—while Garp is writing his third novel *The World According to Bensenhaver*. In order to promote the novel, Garp's editor Wolf markets the work with a reference to Garp being the son of famous feminist Jenny Fields. In order to prevent the resulting hype, the Garps seek temporary shelter in Vienna.

In the meantime, back in the United States, Jenny supports the campaign of the woman candidate for the office of Maine governor. During one of the campaign rallies, Jenny is shot by a deer hunter, who holds Jenny's book responsible for his divorce. Jenny's death prompts the Garp family to return to America. Garp is "supposed" to be excluded from his own mother's funeral, which is arranged by her adherents to be "the first feminist funeral" (Garp 487), where men are not permitted attendance. Garp, disguised as a woman, attends the funeral anyway, but is discovered and has to flee the scene. On his way out, Garp encounters Ellen James, who at eleven had been raped and whose tongue was cut out, so she could not reveal her torturer. She is the eponymous woman for the Ellen Jamesians, who in order to protest against Ellen's fate intentionally cut out their tongues. Ellen actually despises these women, as through her personal tragedy she had been made a public figure by the Ellen Jamesians. Subsequently, Ellen James becomes a dear friend to the Garp family.

Being his mother's heir, Garp takes over her estate at Dog's Head Harbor as well as the Jenny Fields Foundation, which provides women in need with stipends. Upon the death of Helen's father, Garp also becomes the new wrestling coach at Steering school. Garp's and Ellen James' disapproval of the Ellen Jamesians leads to the publication of articles against the movement by Garp and Ellen (*Why I am not an Ellen Jamesian*). Needless to say, Garp becomes the archenemy of the Ellen Jamesians, and one day while jogging, Garp barely escapes an attempted murder by one of them. However, Garp is set up to die due to his public aversion for the radical Ellen Jamesians, and yet Garp's death comes as a surprise. While he is coaching the Steering School's wrestlers in the room in which he fell in love with Helen, he is accosted by "Pooh" Percy—who in the meantime had joined the Ellen Jamesians, and who holds Garp responsible for her sister Cushie's death in delivering her baby. Pooh, disguised as nurse, shoots and kills Garp.

The World According to Garp—as we already can see—is full of existentialist motifs. Clearly, we encounter two existentialist heroes: Jenny Fields and Garp. Both characters can be seen as people who "make" themselves and affirm life as who they are rather than leading a life of accommodation to societal demands and expectations. This becomes particularly clear when looking at the dimensions of everyday morality, bad faith, being-for-others and the character's behavior in an absurd and violent world.

In an existentialist analysis, Garp must be seen as a character, who has mastered the negotiation of past and future, of facticity and transcendence. From early on Garp is someone who is aware of what he is, who knows where he comes from and who is able to conceptualize himself in the future. This becomes particularly obvious, when he decides to become a writer in his teen years. From a Camusean perspective, he certainly is not a procrastinator, who intends to achieve his goals at some point in the future and who will at one point have to reassert his youth as an act of revolt against mortality. Rather, Garp is very much aware of his own mortality from early on and thus works on achieving his goal of becoming a writer during his youth at Steering School. His awareness of mortality, the prospect of death and the longing for a safe space manifests itself when he climbs the roof of the infirmary he grew up in, in order to catch a pigeon, and falls in the roof's rain gutter. It is after his rescue, when he lies in the hospital and for the first time thinks of what will be later called the "Under Toad" (Miller, Irving 97): that "Garp felt a darkness surround him, akin to the darkness and sense of being far way that he must have felt while lying in the rain gutter, four stories above where the world was safe" (Garp 52). Thus, Garp lives consciously from early on, always with the "Under Toad" in mind, the prospect of death in an absurd world becoming his literary motif in writing. Besides deciding to devote his life to writing, Garp also chooses his life-long mate at Steering School. In fact, the mating and the writing go together, as Garp uses writing as a tool to woe young Helen Holm, who will only accept a "true writer" for husband. Garp also engages in wrestling, which

> will metaphorically prepare Garp for the exacting demands of his writing career, but more important, the sport will physically and mentally prepare him for contending with life's disappointments and tragedies, or simply life as a fierce competition and often 'full of disappointment.' (Reilly 72)

His persistence in being confronted with life as such—which can be seen in the context of Camus' revolt against absurdity—manifests itself in his endeavor in "finding his voice, and finding people to listen to it—and hear what he has to say" (Marcus 72). This becomes apparent, when Garp intends to impress Helen with his first story in order to prove his abilities as a writer. Helen sees it at least as a "no-nonsense story"—at bottom a rather disappointing review. Harter and Thompson conclude in this context that "despite Helen's no-nonsense evaluation of the first story he has the temerity to share with her, he is true to his self-described destiny regardless of sacrifices—for himself and others—his choices will exact" (76).

Yet, it is precisely the world's and its inhibitors' cruelty that will influence the course of Garp's writing career. Irving assigns Garp the task "not only to take on the world and understand it but also to re-create it, representing its promises and dangers, in accordance with his own vision" (Miller, Irving 90-91). Revealing and comic at the same time is the description of this process within the novel, when John Wolf, Garp's publisher tells Garp's son Duncan:

> Your father was a difficult fellow; he never gave an inch—but that's the point: he was always following his nose; wherever it took him, it was always *his* nose. And he was ambitious. He started out daring to write about the *world*—when he was just a *kid*, for Christ's sake, he still took it on. Then, for a while—like a lot of writers—he could only write about himself; but he also wrote about the world—it just didn't come through as cleanly. He was starting to get bored with writing about his life and he was beginning to write about the whole world again; he was just starting. (Garp 592)

The World According to Garp presents itself as one, in which human existence is constantly under threat. We are thus not surprised to find that the lives and deaths of the book's characters are constructed as random and absurd. All human beginnings—most certainly Garp's conception comes to mind in this context—and endings present themselves with little logic and subsequently must be seen as senseless. And yet, the set up of the characters' lives seems nothing but a consequence of the postmodern circumstances the novel is set in. Harter and Thompson thus note that Irving "is preeminently a man and writer grounded in the contemporary world where the limitations of knowledge and insight must be embodied and acknowledged even in the most apparently omniscient of voices" (84). The novel's motif, the "Under Toad" in a truly Camusean hostile world, thus becomes accessible from an existentialist viewpoint when considering "the horror stalking the postmodern world [which] is apparent in the number of bizarre, often violent deaths in the plot" (Reilly 63). Irving, throughout the novel gets the reader in a mood, where it is not at all surprising anymore to learn in the epilogue that the Fletchers—whom the Garps were involved with in mate switching—die an absurd death "in their middle age, when their airplane—to Martinique—crashed during the Christmas holiday" (Garp 578). Neither are we surprised that the threatening world at some point will have to cause sorrow and pain for the Garp family. Ironically, the person who invented the "Under Toad" as a family aphorism, Walt, has to die in the car accident following Helen's infidelity. Garp and Jenny Fields have to die absurd deaths as a result of the "ubiquitous 'Under Toad'" (Harter and Thompson 79).

Thus we can understand Garp as a character who encounters a world in which "life is, more than anything else, intense… sharpedged, and dangerous," making the book an account "of the worst fears of its characters coming true" (Marcus 7). It is exactly the absurd nature of this world that attracts Garp as a writer and that imposes difficulty on Garp's endeavor to understand it. A true understanding of the world throughout the novel thus "remains elusive, as Garp is a man surrounded by chaos and violence, which frustrate his search for some pattern of meaning and frequently force his fictions into dead ends and stagnation" (Miller, Irving 91). Particularly, violence adds to the absurdist momentum of the novel, and Marcus attests that the violent motif becomes the adhesive element within *The World According to Garp*, as it "anchors the action and the fate of the characters to a reality outside their own, and it anchors the characters to their own reality" (74).

Nonetheless, Garp finds a *modus vivendi* of dealing with the absurd and violent world—with the "Under Toad." Garp manages coming to terms through fixing his perception "of life's demonic undertow at exactly those points where, any day, any one of us might slip and be sucked down" (Des Pres 32). This manner of dealing with life and the world as they are, in fact, stems from Garp's time in Vienna. In order to absorb the patterns and the meaning of the world—advice Garp had received from his Steering School teacher Mr. Tinch—Garp accompanied by his mother Jenny, absorbs life in Vienna in order to grow as a writer. Vienna, which still suffered from the aftermath of World War II, proved to be the ideal city for Garp to "absorb" life as it stood still for him to examine:

It was Garp's experience to live in a city that made him feel peculiar to be eighteen years old. This must have made him grow older faster, and this must have contributed to his increasing sense that Vienna was more of "a museum housing a dead city"—as he wrote Helen—than it was a city that was still alive.

Garp's observation was not offered as criticism. Garp *liked* wandering around in a museum. "A more real city might not have suited me so well," he later wrote. "But Vienna was in its death phase; it lay still and let me look at it, and think about it, and look again. In a *living* city, I could never have noticed so much. Living cities don't hold still." (Garp 122-123)

Thus, although Garp was never able to achieve a breakthrough in terms of finding any meaning in the world, living in Vienna still "profoundly [affected] his imagination and [helped] form his 'scheme of things'" (Miller, Irving 100). Vienna—being in the process of rising from its ruins—also taught Garp a lesson about the nature of life as he "learns from Vienna's past that there is life after death, that life indeed must go on, and that he must refuse to be victimized by life's forces" (Reilly 62-63).

He also learns how to deal with the "Under Toad" as he encounters the philosophy of Marcus Aurelius, when he buys the English translation of his *Meditations* in a second hand bookstore, because the owner had told Garp that Aurelius had died in Vienna.

"In the life of a man," Marcus Aurelius wrote, "his time is but a moment, his being an incessant flux, his sense a dim rushlight, his body a prey of worms, his soul an unquiet eddy, his fortune dark, his fame doubtful. In short, all that is body is as coursing waters, all that is of the soul as dreams and vapors." Garp somehow thought that Marcus Aurelius must have lived in Vienna when he wrote that. (Garp 126)

Given that Aurelius continues his thought—which is not included in *Garp*—with the idea "the art of living is more like wrestling than dancing, in as much as it, too, demands a firm and watchful stance against any unexpected onset" (Aurelius 115) it will not surprise that

Irving's novel encompasses the duality of Aurelius's problem, the need to structure a world and to maintain vigilance in a world that seems to defy comprehension, the overwhelming need to create or maintain unity out of seeming disunity. (Miller, Irving 93-94)

Inspired by Marcus Aurelius, Garp starts to write his first novel *The Pension Grillparzer*, however he soon discovers that he is not able to finish the story, as he "knew he did not know enough; not yet" (Garp 155).

He put "The Pension Grillparzer"—as they say—aside. It will come, Garp thought. He knew he had to know more; all he could do was look at Vienna and learn. It was holding still for him. Life seemed to be holding still for him. [...] What I need is *vision*, he knew. An overall scheme of things, a vision all his own. [...]
    [...] he knew it would take only time to imagine a world of his own—with a little help from the real world. The real world would soon cooperate. (Garp 155)

Thus Garp evolves himself more and more in his relationship to an older prostitute named Charlotte—adding to his Viennese existentialist experience in the form of a "rarified pleasure" (Harter and Thompson 77)—who is in the process of dying of cancer. It is at this junction that sex and death once again—Garp was conceived by Jenny from a man in the process of dying too—are interwoven. Harter and Thompson thus suggest that the "ironic juxtaposition of sex and death—a juxtaposition central to Irving's vision and native to Vienna—will continue to inspire Garp as artist much as it will haunt him as man" (77). Moreover, from an existentialist viewpoint, and in the upcoming plot of the novel, death plays an integral role in Garp's way of dealing with life. Thus, Charlotte can—according to Miller—be regarded Garp's "spiritual mistress", who as a "proud but aging whore stands as the very embodiment of the city of Vienna, clinging to the memory of a glamorous past, while hiding the scars occasioned by its less glorious moments" (Irving 102). Death and its absurdity had become an integral part of Garp's mindset:

> All around Garp, now, the city looked ripe with dying. The teeming parks and gardens reeked of decay to him, and the subject of the great painters in the great museums was always death. There were always cripples and old people riding the No. 38 Strassenbahn out to Grinzinger Allee, and the heady flowers planted along the pruned paths of the courtyard in the Rudolfinerhaus reminded Garp only of funeral parlors. He recalled the pensions he and Jenny had stayed in when they first arrived, over a year ago: the faded and unmatched wallpaper, the dusty bric-a-brac, the chipped china, the hinges crying for oil. "In the life of a man," wrote Marcus Aurelius, "his time is but a moment... his body a prey of worms...." (Garp 163)

Nonetheless, the way Irving (respectively Garp) deals with the prospect of death appears in a comic way, in which dying appears as something to be scorned. Miller thus attests that "Irving declare[s his] freedom from the specter of death by laughing at it and playing with it, [...] dealing with bizarre events and insisting that laughter is a 'species of sympathy'" (Irving 97). What could be more bizarre than a protagonist bonding with a dying prostitute—claiming to be her son while she is fading away in a hospital. It has to be seen in the context of laughing at death that "Garp, because he lives in a violent [and absurd] world, learns from his experiences and develops a positive code for living purposefully despite life's sometimes overwhelming forces" (Reilly 65).

Garp derives meaning from his life in dedicating himself to others—showing solidarity with those who are confronted with violence and the prospect of death in this very absurd world. This becomes particularly clear within the family sphere, most prominent when dealing with the vulnerability and mortality of his own sons:

> It had been an unpleasant sensation for Garp, shortly after Duncan turned six, to smell that Duncan's breath was stale and faintly foul in his sleep. It was as if the process of decay, of slowly dying, was already begun in him. This was Garp's first awareness

of the mortality of his son. There appeared with this odor the first discolorations and strains on Duncan's perfect teeth. Perhaps it was just that Duncan was Garp's firstborn child, but Garp worried more about Duncans than he worried about Walt—even though a five-year-old seems more prone (than a ten-year-old) to the usual childhood accidents. And what are *they*? Garp wondered. Being hit by cars? Choking to death on peanuts? Being stolen by strangers? Cancer, for example, was a stranger.

There was so much to worry about, when worrying about children, and Garp worried so much about everything; at times, especially in these throes of insomnia, Garp thought himself to be psychologically unfit for parenthood. (Garp 275)

Another of the novel's characters—Jenny Fields—is also worried about the growing up of her child Garp. She, too is an overprotective parent, who studies various sports in order to find the right one for Garp, and—while being the school nurse—attends classes at Steering School in order to determine what Garp should take once he reaches schooling age. Particularly her choosing wrestling for Garp is symbolic within the context of the novel. Although wrestling appears to be a violent sport, it will not only "prepare Garp for the exacting demands of his writing career [and ...] life's disappointments and tragedies" (Reilly 72), and make Garp a stronger person, but the wrestling room also appeared to her to be "padded against pain" (Garp 85). It seems that Garp inherits the protective spirit from his mother and Miller suggests that the protagonist thus "emerges gradually as a true hero in an age without heroes, for his life is an obsessive attempt to make a threatening world safe for his children" (Irving 90). It is thus not surprising to have Irving let Garp check on his son while sleeping over at a friend's or have Garp get into a fight with a speeding plumber whom he sees a threat to the children in the neighborhood.

Another dimension of the "Under Toad" is opened up through rape, which is a consistent and strong theme throughout *The World According to Garp*. The portrayal of rape in the novel as a result of "life's overwhelming forces" allows for the novel's characters to demonstrate solidarity with affected women as a form of rebellion against absurdity. Rape, as a symbol of an absurd and violent world in all its ugliness, according to Irving, is a "central crime. It's probably the most violent assault on the body and the head that can happen simultaneously—that doesn't kill you" (Greil, The World of 74). It represents "the whole area of anarchy, chaos, viciousness, and amorality" (Ibid 73); and Garp as well as Jenny Fields will become involved in the issue. The evils of the world thus are "identified with amorality (not the refusal of morals, but their absolute absence) and represented by rapists" (Greil, Death 8).

Both characters' involvement with rape and subsequently the feminist movement starts when Jenny writes her autobiography in Vienna, which later became known as "the first truly feminist autobiography." Despite the fact that Jenny constantly "claims [not to be] a women liberationist, she becomes one of the feminist movement's champions because of her book" (Reilly 66).

Not being able to prevent herself being

> adopted as a heroine by various women's groups all over the country and [being] considered a guru by others, [Jenny who is ministrative] by nature as well as by training [as a nurse], [...] responds to her celebrity status by taking in victims of rape and trying to help as many women as she can, although she remains uncomfortable in her role as a "feminist." (Miller, Irving 108)

Jenny Fields is in two aspects a particularly interesting character from an existentialist viewpoint. First, her being-for-other's, and second her non-conformism—or rather—her being free from everyday morality. Thinking in terms of being-for-others, Jenny Fields clearly has been "gazed upon" as a feminist. Her refusal to share her body with a man, and her willingness to work with women who had been hurt or have to suffer, are considered traits of a feminist. However, we learn that Jenny fields has enormous difficulty with being considered a feminist. A scene after Jenny's death, in which Garp, Roberta (a transsexual family friend and former Philadelphia Eagles tight end) and Jenny's editor John Wolf meet, illustrates the problematic issue of being-for-others:

48

"Did you ever see that thing she wrote about being called a feminist?" Roberta and John Wolf looked at each other; they looked stricken and gray. "She said, 'I hate being called one, because it's a label I didn't choose to describe my feelings about men or the way I write.

"I don't want to argue with you, Garp," Roberta said. "Not now. You know perfectly well she said other things, too. She *was* a feminist, whether she liked the label or not. She was simply for allowing women to live their own lives and make their own choices." (Garp 488-489)

Jenny Field's non-self-identification as a feminist also becomes clear when she tries to comfort her grandson Duncan after he has lost his eye in the car crash during Helen's breaking up with her student:

It was with his grandmother, Jenny Fields, that Duncan would see his first glass eye. "See?" Jenny said. "It's big and brown; it's not quite as pretty as your left one, but you just make sure the girls see your left one first." It was not a very feminist thing to say, she supposed, but Jenny always said that she was, first and foremost, a nurse. (Garp 375-376)

Yet, Jenny Field's reluctance to identify herself as a feminist stems from her desire to be true to herself. As Miller notes:

Being in tune with one's own nature and living according to it in one's own world is a major theme in *Garp*, and Jenny Fields, fiercely independent, does indeed create her own world. As a child she studied clams—"It was the first live thing she understood completely—its life, its sex, its death"—and when she becomes a nurse, she discovers "that people weren't much more mysterious, or more attractive than clams." Having dealt with pregnant women who did not want their babies and with diseases, she develops a strong distaste for sex and decides to live a life without sex. (Irving 94)

In existentialist perspective, Jenny Field's refusal to being labeled a feminist, can be seen as a successful attempt not to fall into Sartre's bad faith. Although certain character traits and behaviorisms of

Jenny Fields indeed remind very much of a feminist woman per se, she would rather remain a nurse, instead of "falling" into being identified a feminist and thus she succeeds in remaining authentic. Jenny Fields, in actually *being and remaining* a nurse—long after she quit her job and began to shelter women in need—can be seen as a strong woman, having "very certain ideas about the rights of the individual and those of women in particular" (McKay 83). Jenny's appreciation of an individual's rights become apparent in her adolescent years, when "her fierce non-conformity and independence—from most men and from the largely hypocritical values of a New England upperclass family—is instantly evoked by her joint desires to work in a declassé profession of nursing and to have a baby without the acceptable accoutrements" (Harter and Thompson 75).

Revisiting the issue of rape—which will allow us to deal with the Ellen Jamesians in-depth—Garp's experience with rape stems on the one hand, of course, from being Jenny Field's son; being the 'being-for-other's feminist's' son "Garp has been exposed to female suffering for most of his life" (McKay 84). On the other hand, Garp has his own experiences with rape—most importantly when he finds a ten year old girl in the park who had just been raped, and he was made "a 'hero' for swiftly apprehending the rapist" (Harter and Thompson 78). Yet although being a hero, this incident makes Garp feel responsible:

> "I feel uneasy," Garp wrote, "that my life has come in contact with so much rape." Apparently, he was referring to the ten-year-old in the city park, to the eleven-year-old Ellen James and her terrible society—his mother's wounded women with their symbolic, self-inflicted speechlessness. And later he would write a novel, which would make Garp more of "a household product," which would have much to do with rape. Perhaps rape's offensiveness to Garp was that it was an act that disgusted him with himself—with his own very male instincts, which were otherwise so unassailable. He never felt like raping everyone; but rape, Garp thought, made men feel guilt by association. (Garp 209)

Garp's existence in "Irving's world [that] embraces sexual equality and androgyny" (Rickard 715) on the one hand, while being confronted with gender brutality on the other hand. This manifests itself not only in the rape/male sexuality issue but even more so in Garp's relationship with pseudo-feminist movements. Thus it is not surprising that Garp "engages in a love-hate relationship with a variety of feminist types, many of whom quickly identify him [ironically] as the enemy." Although Garp is a hero due to his catching a rapist, although he is Jenny Field's son and although he is liberal in attitudes, he "is nevertheless despised and ridiculed by lunatic fringe feminists who have cut out their own tongues in stupid acts of symbolic identification with a rape and mutilation victim named Ellen James" (Harter and Thompson 78). Garp's sympathy for the Ellen Jamesians thus amounts to zero, while he is compassionate with Ellen James herself.

>Garp would see more of the Ellen Jamesians. Although he felt deeply disturbed by what had happened to Ellen James, he felt only disgusted at her grown-up, sour imitators whose habit was to present you with a card. [...]
>
>The Ellen Jamesians represented, for Garp, the kind of women who lionized his mother and sought to use her to help further their crude causes.
>
>"I'll tell you something about those women, Mom," he said to Jenny once. "They were probably all lousy at talking, anyway; they probably never had a worthwhile thing to say in their lives—so their tongues were no great sacrifice; in fact, it probably saves them considerable embarrassment. If you see what I mean."
>
>"You're a little short on sympathy," Jenny told him.
>
>"I have *lots* of sympathy—for Ellen James," Garp said.
>
>"These women must have suffered, in other ways, themselves," Jenny said. "That's what makes them want to get closer to each other."
>
>"And inflict more suffering on themselves, Mom?"
>
>"Rape is every woman's problem," Jenny said. Garp hated his mother's "everyone" language most of all. A case, he thought, of carrying democracy to an idiotic extreme.
>
>"It's every man's problem, too, Mom. The next time there's a rape, suppose I cut my *prick* off and wear it around my neck. Would you respect *that*, too?"
>
>"We're talking about *sincere* gestures," Jenny said.
>
>"We're talking about *stupid* gestures," Garp said. (Garp 191-192)

Marcus writes about the Ellen Jamesians that they "are the most disturbing and pathetic presence in the book. They are the adversaries of Garp, Helen and Roberta; the friends of Jenny Fields, who takes them in as she takes in all female strays who come to her" (5). From an existentialist viewpoint, ignorant feminism—such as the one exercised by the Ellen Jamesians—amounts to a betrayal of solidarity in the absurd world.

In other words:

> With death awaiting us, loss and fear part of our lives, we need no additional threats, but we have them anyway: they are sex, violence and feminism, which Irving seems to conflate. In other words, he seems to believe that feminism is a violent response to male sexuality. [...] scores of women celebrate Ellen James by cutting out their own tongues, and banding together in hatred of men. [...] The behavior of these women lacks what another T.S. called objective correlative:[11] their revenge is out of all proportion to the "insult." (French 75)

Garp's problem with the Ellen Jamesians can also be approached from a perspective on perversion, something Garp cannot accept. Miller argues that Garp's "anger at the Ellen Jamesians is [...] justified because if the perversion of sex is rape, the perversion of language is propaganda, hysteria and other forms of voicelessness" (Irving 108-109). Instead of recognizing the creative potential of language, the Ellen Jamesians misuse and abuse this "connective force" and make their self-mutilation a most "powerful divisive" (Miller, Irving 108-109) influence. No wonder thus they "let Garp seethe. What else could they do? It was not one of Garp's better points: tolerance of

---

[11] T.S. Eliot

the intolerant. Crazy people made him crazy" (McKay 87). Garp, although he certainly is a rather non-political person rejects "the maniacal adherence to a cause or idea, to the exclusion of everything else" (Campbell 79)—commonly referred to as ideology. Ultimately Garp's rejection of the Ellen Jamesians' capitalization on Ellen's pain for their own purposes and his subsequent "opposition to the fanaticism of the Ellen Jamesians" (Ibid) will partly lead to his assassination by Pooh Percy, who in the course of the novel 'converts' to Ellen Jamesianism, still holding Garp—for irrational reasons—responsible for her sister Cushie's death.[12]

The threat of fanaticism, which adds up to the already existing 'Under Toad,' in *The World According to Garp*, however, also comes from the other direction, giving the theme a more holistic profile within the novel. It is the fact that Jenny Fields is shot at an election rally in New Hampshire by a deer hunter, who holds her responsible for his ex-wife divorcing him, that allows for irony and absurdity to show once more. Reilly thus concludes: "A man who hates women kills Jenny, and a woman who hates men kills Garp; these assassins personify what Irving labels the 'contemporary fascist spirit'" (73). In this context, it appears tempting to argue that the Ellen Jamesians—contrary to Jenny Fields—have fallen into bad faith through this very fascist spirit. It appears that these women rather than engaging in what Jenny Fields does—helping others in a violent and absurd world—just love to *play* their roles as 'radical feminists,' not *caring* about real feminist issues.

At this point, we shall turn to an existentialist examination of sexuality as portrayed in *The World According to Garp*. In existentialist perspective, the novel provides two important aspects on the issue. First, Garp clearly is a Dun Juanesque character and second, the way the Garps and other characters deal with their sexuality allows for an analysis within the being-for-others dimension.

---

[12] French notes in this context that Irving is being unrealistic in the plot at this point, as women "do not act this way on the whole. Those who martyr themselves do it instead of opposing men, not *in order* to oppose them. It is unlikely that a woman would murder the child of a woman who took her in, tried to heal her, offered her understanding and love—however she felt about that child" (76).

The existentialist dimension of Garp's sexuality becomes apparent from early on in the novel. Garp loses his virginity with Cushie Percy, setting the path for Garp's sexual future, which will take him via an affair with a prostitute into the marital domain with Helen Holms. However, Garp subsequently is not able to limit his sexual adventures to his wife, as his desire will be directed towards baby-sitters and diverse other women he meets. The nature of Garp's sexual desires is shaped by his experience with Cushie Percy—taking place in the Steering School's infirmary—opening up the full existentialist discourse of sex in an absurd world:

> [... Sex] for Garp would forever be associated with certain smells and sensations. The experience would remain secretive but relaxed: a final reward in harrowing times. The odor would stay in his mind as deeply personal and yet vaguely *hospital*. The surroundings would forever seem to be deserted. Sex for Garp would remain in his mind as a solitary act committed in an abandoned universe—sometime after it had rained. It was always an act of terrific optimism. (Garp 114)

Clearly, sex for Garp becomes a life-affirming act in the absurd world, fulfilling Camus' characterization of the Don Juan, being someone who "loves [the women] with the same passion and each time with his whole self that he must repeat his gift and his profound quest" (Camus 67). In the novel it becomes implicitly and explicitly obvious that Garp is passionate with all the women he has intercourse with, and Harter and Thompson argue in this context that the manner of Garp's initiation into the sexual world "will ultimately shape his entire adult experience, [being ...] one of the ways the world according to Irving is given existential and artistic form" (76). Although his flings with baby-sitters seem unimportant, they are not—Garp thinks about them throughout the novel. Even with Charlotte—the Viennese prostitute—Garp is wholeheartedly involved, even going so far as to claim that she is his mother while Charlotte is dying in a hospital. In his adult experience, however, sexuality is always conflated with male guilt, something which makes his Don Juanism somewhat complicated. Harter and Thompson note that "Garp is thrust into a world where

54

women dominate his life and consciousness and where acute awareness of the victimization of women—most potently symbolized by rape—is, for him, in constant and irresolvable tension with the lust he continues to feel" (78). This becomes particularly apparent in his sexual flings with the family's baby-sitters:

> [Garp] likened his guilt for the seduction of Little Squab Bones to a rapelike situation. But it was hardly a rape. It was deliberate, though. He even bought the condoms weeks in advance, knowing what he would use them for. Are not the worst crimes premeditated? It would not be a sudden passion for the baby-sitter that Garp would succumb to; he would plan, and be ready when Cindy succumbed to *her* passion for him. (Garp 209)

In a mate swapping episode involving the Garps and the Fletchers (another university couple), Garp's and to some extent all of the involved people's Don Juanesque behavior surfaces. However, Reilly notes: "During the mate swapping, Garp and Alice love each other, and Harrison loves Helen, but, [...] Helen does not fall in love" (68).

At this point, Garp and Helen [not quite yet] become existentialist heroes on another note, as they become aware of the possibility of mechanisms of sadism and masochism. Everybody, except for Helen, is in love—in terms of Sartre's being-for-others, they are reaffirmed in their identities, in what they really are—and thus the mate swapping is the right thing for them to do. It is thus unsurprisingly "Helen [who] terminates this quaternation because she enjoys 'it the least of them' and 'suffered the most'" (Reilly 68), ultimately restoring her freedom from "being absorbed" by the others involved.

Being bored a little later with the relationship with Garp, Helen, however, initiates an affair with Michael Milton, her student, which will become the final straw of infidelities in the marriage. It appears that she "maintains this relationship, because she controls it" (Reilly 68), again reminding us about the existentialist concept of sadism—now with Helen in charge, and Michael Milton trying to win her over. It is when she realizes that Garp is aware of this affair and hurt, that she terminates it. What Reilly sees in this context as ironic—that Garp and Helen "become aware at this juncture of how much they love each other" (65)—does only seem logical from an existentialist viewpoint. It rather is *because* of Garp being deeply hurt, that the couple is able to reaffirm their love for each other—which is certainly a true one—finally escaping the vicious circle of sadism and masochism. Even the death of their son Walt in the process of Helen breaking up with Michael Milton cannot harm their relationship anymore as "their love deepens and transcends this tragedy" (Ibid 68).

In this context—bringing together the dimension of human solidarity within an absurd world and the disappointments of human interaction—faith in each other and a life affirming attitude become particularly important. Thus Marcus suggests that the "struggle defined in *Garp* is not the hopeless struggle of men and women to beat the Reaper (as 'We are all terminal cases' seems to imply), but the struggle of certain men and women to keep faith in each other" (8). Miller detects a parallel between Garp and Laurence Sterne's Tristram Shandy [T.S. !!!] in this context, as both protagonists' worlds are "full of violent incident and fatality—the concentration on physical maiming is particularly noticeable—and yet both writers place primary emphasis on the constructive feelings of their characters and the spirit of affirmation inherent in their behavior" (Irving 96). This constructiveness in the behavior of the novel's characters is truly interesting from an existentialist perspective. As Marcus notes, "to say that these people are good is not to say that they're benign, or that their struggle to keep faith in each other isn't marked—even shaped by betrayals" (73). It appears that their consciousness in dealing with others is what allows them to continue having faith in each other. In reference to the Sartrean being-for-others the statement—that each "of these people is to some degree apart from the others, from all others: they love, they are devoted, but they are incapable of surrender to anyone else. The connections they make to others are deep, but on their own terms" (Marcus 73)—sheds light on the relationships in the novel. It seems that the characters in *The World According to Garp* are somehow aware of their being-for-others as they "recognize the tension between themselves and their family, and try to walk the line" (Ibid). However—and this is where the element of solidarity resolves the dilemma created by being-for-others—the novel's existentialist heroes never "do the prudent thing and shrivel up inside [and refuse] to block out the world and wall themselves off with egotism" (Ibid). It can be seen in this light that both—Garp and Helen—are able to overcome the loss of their son Walt and to save their relationship. While Garp uses art for reconciliation with the "real and terrible world" (Garp 442) through writing *The World According to Bensenhaver*, Helen reconciles "herself to the past [through making] an affirmative commitment: she and Garp have another child, a daughter whom they aptly name Jenny Garp" (Harter and Thompson 80). Again, we detect an existentialist exploit with both protagonists, as they are able to cope with the past (facticity) and are able to envision a meaningful future (transcendence). Out of experience, Garp and Helen develop their own sense of the right thing to do—to live up to a self-defined morality. This life-affirming moral at bottom might be identified with managing "to live in their own worlds without refusing to live in those of others—without denigrating them" (Marcus 72).

Thus, towards the end of the novel, we cannot be really surprised that Garp also comes to terms with the Ellen Jamesians. It is at his mother's feminist funeral, which he has to attend disguised as a woman, that he experiences what it must be like to be a woman. Moreover, the Garps befriend Ellen James herself, and these two instances trigger "the transformation of the central figure [...] about sexual strife and true liberation" (Miller, Irving 113).

Parallel to Roberta Muldoon's liberation from her killer instinct—the remainder from her former football career—Garp is also able to "overcome [the] impulsive aggression in himself" (Miller, Irving 122)—something "basically male and basically intolerant" (Garp 556) that the Ellen Jamesians had sensed in him. Truly ironic though, that after this successful transformation through finding "his maturity in making a total commitment to the life-affirming values of family and responsibility" (Miller, Irving 121), Garp is shot by Pooh Percy in the wrestling room—which had been intended to be padded against pain.

However, Irving has prepared us for Garp's violent death as in "the world according to Garp, an evening could be hilarious and the next morning could be murderous" (Garp 565).

3.3. The Hotel New Hampshire

The family epic *The Hotel New Hampshire* stretches from the beginning of the 1940s to the late 1970s and comprises three generations. Taking the perspective of John Berry, the narrative unfolds around the childhood and adolescence of the five Berry children.

In the manner of a genesis and as a cohesive element throughout the novel—Campbell (88) and Miller (Irving 129), for instance refer to *The Hotel New Hampshire* as a fairy tale—the plot starts off with the encounter of Winslow Berry and Mary Bates who meet at the Arbuthnot-by-the-Sea in the summer of 1939, where they are employed as seasonal workers. We meet another character, Freud, an Austrian Jew who entertains the hotel's guest with his bear. It is he who initiates the upcoming marriage, as he convinces the couple to marry immediately. Freud, after being offended by German Nazis in the hotel, returns to Austria in order to "find a more clever bear," despite the Nazi-regime already being in place. Win inherits Freud's bear and the motorcycle and finances his studies at Harvard University through these assets.

Soon, the Berrys become the parents of three children: Frank, Franny and John. Win graduates from Harvard and is drafted by the army in World War II, which he survives. Later, Lilly and Egg are born, while the family lives in Mary's deceased parents' house and Win teaches at the local Dairy School. Iowa Bob, Win's father, and Sorrow, the family dog, are at this point introduced to the plot.

However, since the summer at the Arbuthnot, Win Berry cannot let go of the thought of running a hotel by himself and subsequently convinces his family to turn a former girl's school into the first Hotel New Hampshire, which will act "as a safe space for the children" (Campbell 90). At the first Hotel Hampshire the reader becomes familiar with the tumultuous episodes surrounding the family and the everyday school lives of the children at the Dairy School. We encounter strange and unpleasant incidents and developments, which the Berry children are confronted with. Franny is gang raped by some members of the Dairy School's football team under the "leadership" of quarterback Chipper Dove, and an attempted rescue by the team's black players fails. Frank, the oldest son is discovering his homosexuality and is subsequently mobbed at the school. John is approaching his sexuality through "somewhat unsatisfactory sex with Ronda Ray" (Campbell 91), who is the hotel's maid. The children's beloved dog Sorrow "is put to sleep, primarily because he 'smelled bad,' 'farted' and 'defecated' on the floor" (Ibid), forever associating his death with the rape of Franny, since the two events occurred simultaneously. Yet, another death is to come: Frank, who recently took a taxidermy class, stuffs Sorrow as a Christmas present for Egg. However, Iowa Bob—who had been the family's calming influence—encounters the stuffed Sorrow when opening his closet and dies from a heart attack.

Upon the receipt of a letter from Freud—who finally found a clever "bear"— requesting the Berrys to come to Vienna in order to run his "deluxe-class possibility" (Hotel 223) Gasthaus Freud and to restore its glory days, the family prepares to depart for Austria. The Berrys who are not particularly excited about the prospect of moving to Vienna—with the exception of Frank who is interested in Vienna's history—fly to Europe in two separate planes. Unsurprisingly—since it is Irving's writing we are dealing with here—the plane in which Mother, Egg and the stuffed Sorrow travel crashes, and Mother and Egg die.

Arriving in Vienna, the grief-stricken Berrys encounter an amaurotic Freud, who lost his eyesight in a Nazi concentration camp, and his bear Susie—who in fact is a young woman dressed as a bear. The soon renamed "Hotel New Hampshire" is inhabited by five prostitutes on one floor and a gang of six political radicals—who soon will engage in terrorism—without a clear political aim, on the other. Soon, the children and Susie—who just like Franny, had been a rape victim—grow very close, Franny and Susie even engaging sexually and temporarily becoming a couple. One of the young radicals, Fräulein Fehlgeburt, not only reads *The Great Gatsby* and *Moby Dick* to the children, but also engages sexually with John. Things, however, turn out to be complicated, as John has been secretly in love with his sister Franny for the longest time. The older female radical *Schwangere* also gets close to the Berry children, who have been half-orphans since the plane crash over the Atlantic ocean, in a motherly way.

Freud's vision of Win Berry turning the run-down Gasthaus Freud into a fine hotel, becomes frustrated as the *Hotel New Hampshire* remains run-down and the guests remain the same. However, the children develop into young adults during the seven years in Vienna. Lilly—who is of dwarfish statue—even manages to "grow a little" (which becomes a family aphorism) through writing her first autobiographical novel, which is published with the help of Frank. The family's stay in Vienna ends abruptly, when the radicals plan to undertake a terror attack at the Vienna Opera House. The Berrys are able to prevent the attack, but they have to pay a price. Win Berry is left blind, Freud dies in the process.

Since the family is financially secure due to the success of Lilly's novel, they are able to go back to the United States and take Susie with them. Again, the family finds itself in a hotel—the New York based Stanhope—while its members try to balance their lives again. John and Franny finally let every restriction go, and excessively let their lust for each other loose in order to bring their infatuation for each other to an end. In the meantime, Lilly is unsuccessfully trying to write her second novel.

Also in New York the Berrys encounter two people from their past again. Junior Jones, who was leading the unsuccessful rescue mission when Franny was raped, is now courting Franny, and Chipper Dove, Franny's rapist. Moreover, the Berry children together with Susie take revenge for Franny's rape in a surreal manner, as they threaten Chipper Dove to be raped by "bear" Susie.

In the end we learn about the fate of the Berry family members. Win Berry still dreams about his dream hotel, and due to the money Lilly has earned as an author, the children buy the Arbuthnot-by-the-sea for him. John moves in with Win, who is led to believe that he is living in a luxury hotel that can afford to be run although there are not many guests. Lilly's process of growing comes to an abrupt end when she decides to jump from the 14th floor of the Stanhope and ends her life—because she "never grew big enough to write" (Hotel 419). However, there is a scurrile happy ending: Franny finally marries Junior Jones, while John and Susie end up in a happy relationship. The book concludes thus on a happy note: "In the Hotel New Hampshire, we're screwed down for life—but what's a little air in the pipes, or even a lot of shit in the hair, if you have good memories?" (Ibid 418).

In *Hotel New Hampshire*, we once again encounter a world, which is full of absurdity at its best and in which the novel's protagonists are in the process of finding ways to deal with it in a positive manner. However, and this is the novel's literary motif, the protagonists deal with a society that "has stifled man's basic instincts and drives" (Miller, Irving 138). Symbolically thus, the bear State O'Maine is kept by the Berry family in their hotel—and it the Berry family who has to find resolutions within the grotesque modern-day society.

As already stated above, the fairy tale structure of the novel starts with Mother and Father meeting in a still intact world at the dawn of World War II. The absurd world, however, manifests not only in the happenings around World War II throughout the novel, but also representatively when the bear State O'Maine is killed on the Arbuthnot-by-the Sea's pier by a young boy, an act which "symbolizes the postmodern world's sudden, absurd violence" (Reilly 82). It is also in the context of the bear's death, that the decline of Father's illusions of establishing his family in a perfect world in the hotel business begins. Miller (Irving 145) argues in this context that

> John's first memory, thus, is one of loss. His father—a stranger to the children since he has always been away, on the road or at school—mourns the corpse of his illusions, forever oblivious of the precariousness of his position and to the danger nearby.

Mother can only comfort the children, while Father clutches at his dreams, unable to let go.

However, Irving has prepared us for the destruction of perfect-world-illusions and the downfall of the 'old world' as we learned that Freud, in trying to escape Nazi-Austria, had to encounter racists in the United States—prompting him to return to Austria. At this point the Berrys are exposed to the ills of public life as they are "beset by both racists and by enraged victims of racism" (DeMott 14).

However, as in *The World According to Garp*, Irving provides his protagonists with a safe space within the unfolding absurd and hostile world. Thus, as Miller (Irving 152) suggests, Coach Bob's room—similarly to the wrestling room in *Garp*—turns into "a sanctuary and a place of peace, like a womb within a womb" for John. Moreover, the whole family is kept safe at least in the first Hotel New Hampshire, whereas the world outside presents itself as dangerous and violent. The hotel ceases to be a safe space, however, when Frank decides to stuff the family's dead dog Sorrow and brings him into the family home. Coach Bob's fatal heart attack is directly linked to Sorrow's appearance in the hotel: While Coach Bob is working out in his room together with John, the dog falls out of Coach Bob's closet—where Sorrow was hidden since he was intended to be a Christmas present for Egg, the family's youngest—and shocks Coach Bob who dies of a heart attack. From then on, "life is not wholly peaceful" (Miller, Irving 152) anymore for the Berry family, and the absurd world manifests itself tragically for every single family member.

Sorrow subsequently becomes a family euphemism for all upcoming events that will befall the family. The flatulent Labrador Retriever "who dies but does not disappear, the free-floating dog of anxiety whose remains come to the surface even after the airplane he rides in plunges into the sea" (Shostak, Repetition 101), is bound to constantly accompany the Berrys—no matter whether physically or metaphorically. Shostak suggests that "Sorrow is the return of the repressed, punning reminder and even cause of the violence that is our human lot, [...] and his visitations provide a symbolic structure of the Berry family's lives" (Ibid).

The outside world impacts deeply on the Berry's. And once again, sexuality, violence and death are linked in Irving's work. Coach Bob's death, for example is linked with the gang rape inflicted on Franny. As Miller notes in this context, Franny is at the center of the Berry children's sexual escapades: "All are violent confrontations, and all are associated with either death or excrement, or both. Thus, in the trio's adolescent experience, sexual violence, excretion, and death are linked" (Irving 148-149). As the plot progresses, the Berrys' relocation to Vienna will not change this intermingling of the above noted themes. On the way to Europe, Mother and Egg die in a plane crash and upon arrival in Vienna, the Berrys' encounter with the absurd is about to intensify. Thus we are not surprised to learn, that the *Gasthaus Freud* , which will become the second Hotel New Hampshire is inhabited by prostitutes and terrorists. It is in Vienna, where the final violence of the novel is about to take place (Ibid 164-165).

If we analyze *The Hotel New Hampshire* in terms of its fairy tale-like structure, with the trinity of separation (we shall remember that Mother and Egg died on the journey), initiation and return (cf. Miller, Irving 133: Campbell's "monomyth"), the family's stay in Vienna can be seen as the children's initiation phase as "they descend into a strange world and learn lessons there that will help them upon their return" (Miller, Irving 154). And indeed, the Vienna the Berrys encounter in the 1950s[13] could not be a better place for them in order to be confronted with absurdity:

> [...] Between the airport and the outer districts, we passed a Russian tank that had been firmly arranged—in concrete—as a kind of memorial. The tank's top hatch was sprouting flowers, its long barrel was draped with flags, its red star faded and speckled by

---

[13] It is interesting to note here that Irving chose Vienna for personal, not literary reasons (he studied there as a young man), although Vienna seems to be the perfect place in the context of the plot. Thunecke (277) notes: "The Berrys' 'American Dream' of a world inhabited by blissful innocence would therefore have turned into a nightmare just about *anywhere else* abroad; however, Irving—as in the plot of his previous novels—chose to inextricably link this 'dream'—and its violent conclusion—to the decadence of the *Austrian* capital's *fin-de-siècle* era [...]."

birds. It was permanently parked in front of what looked like a post office, but our cab flew by too fast for us to be sure.

Sorrow floats, but we arrived in Vienna before our bad news arrived, and we were inclined toward a cautious optimism. The war damage was more contained as we approached the inner districts; on occasion, even the sun shone through the elaborate buildings—and a row of stone cupids leaned off a roof over us, their bellies pockmarked by machine-gun fire. More people appeared in the streets, though the outer districts resembled one of those old sepia photographs taken at a time of day before everyone was up—or after everyone had been killed. (Hotel 218)

The family is awaited by Freud in Vienna, and we learn that he survived a Nazi death camp, having been blinded by an 'experiment' during his captivity. Thus Freud with his horrible experiences turns into "another reminder of the *Anschluss*-spawned violence" (Reilly 83). He functions as somewhat of a "tour guide" for the Berry family in an absurd and fatal world:

> We were in the Judenplatz, the old Jewish quarter of the city. It had been a kind of ghetto as long ago as the thirteenth century; the first expulsion of the Jews, there, had been in 1421. We knew only slightly more about the recent expulsion.
>
> What was hard about being there with Freud was that this tour was not so visibly historical. Freud would call out to apartments that were no longer apartments. He would identify whole buildings that were no longer there. And the *people* he used to know there—they weren't there, either. It was a tour of things we couldn't see, but Freud saw them still; he saw 1939, and before, when he'd last been in the Judenplatz with a working pair of eyes. (Hotel 270)

The misery the children encounter in Vienna and their own personal issues—Lilly being dwarfish, Frank being homosexual, Franny having been raped—create an emotional hullabaloo. However, the children still manage to regard themselves as ordinary children, although neither their "environment nor their individual natures quite warrant those labels" (DeMott 14).

"You see," Franny would explain, years later, "we *aren't* eccentric, we're *not* bizarre. To each other," Franny would say, "we're as common as rain." And she was right: to each other, we were as normal and nice as the smell of bread, we were just a family. In a family, even exaggerations make perfect sense; they are always *logical* exaggerations, nothing more. (Hotel 161)

However, one family member—Lilly—completely drifts into—what Frank would describe as—*Weltschmerz*. She is bound to never fulfill the family's dictum of her just having to "grow." Not only is she overwhelmed by the appearances of postwar Vienna and the horrible history she encounters there—the Holocaust being the climax of an absurd world—but she also cannot deal "with the politics of sex of the second hotel" (Miller, Irving 160). Moreover, Lilly never receives the kind of positive criticism for her literary work she would need to become more confident. Bowers Hill suggests on this note that Lilly "finally feels she must die, being unable 'to grow enough' to write the kind of book that would win the approval she needs" (69).

While Lilly, retreats from the absurd world, John on the other hand engages in it, and learns his lessons from it. While being in love with his sister Franny, he visits some of the prostitutes who live in the second Hotel New Hampshire. However, "John unconsciously realizes that he will need a more fulfilling sexual relationship before he can grow" (Miller, Irving 159). He tries to establish such a relationship with one of the terrorists—Fehlgeburt—once again directing the plot towards the absurd intermingling of sex and death. It is in the night when Fehlgeburt confides in John about their plans to blow up the Vienna Opera, that the two of them finally make love. However, it is not an act of lust, but rather Fehlgeburt regards this sexual encounter as a life experience she wants to have before she dies. Unsurprisingly, John cannot enjoy sex with Fehlgeburt as it "was as desperate and joyless as any sex in the second Hotel New Hampshire ever was" (Hotel 290). When later that night, Fehlgeburt dies in the terror attack on the opera, it becomes clear that sex in the hotel as well as the radicals are "thematically implicated with death. Both are antilife, and anitlove" (Miller, Irving 159).

It is in this context that the existentialist notions of bad-faith and being-for-others once again surface in Irving's writing, when considering the roles the radicals and the prostitutes take up in the novel:

> [... Despite] their day-and-night differences, they bore more similarities to each other than *they* might have supposed.
> They both believed in the commercial possibilities of a simple ideal: they both believed they could, one day, be "free." They both though that their own bodies were objects easily sacrificed for a cause (and easily restored, or replaced, after the hardship for sacrifice). Even their names were similar—if for different reasons. They had only code names, or nicknames, or if they used their real names, they used only their first names.
> Two of them actually shared the same name, but there was no confusion, since the radical was male, the whore was female, and they were never at the Gasthaus Freud at the same time. [...] The oldest whore was called this because her prices were substandard for the district of the city she strolled [...].
> Her namesake, among the radicals, was the old gentleman who had argued most ferociously with Freud about moving to the fifth floor. *This* Old Billig had earned his "cheap" designation for his reputation of leading a hand-to-mouth existence—and his history of being what the other radicals called "a radical's radical." When there were Bolsheviks, he was one; when the names changed, he changed his name. He was at the forefront of every movement, but—somehow—when the movement ran amok or into terminal trouble, Old Billig took up the rear position and discreetly trailed away out of sight, waiting for the next forefront. The idealists among the younger radicals were both suspicious of Old Billig and admiring of his endurance—his survival. This was not unlike the view held of Old Billig, the whore, by *her* colleagues. (Hotel 230-231)

In a meta perspective, it is us—the readers—who gaze upon the prostitutes as well as on the radicals, so "they are for us," and Irving assigns them with names, that are emblematically in the light of being-for-others: Screaming Annie, Arbeiter, Wrench, and so forth—not allowing for insight into their personalities underneath the surface. However, this is obviously Irving's intention, in order to portray the "simplicity of their ideals and the illusion of possible 'freedom' readily mark these two bands of freaks as aberrant specimen, [...] irresponsible purveyors of the commodities of sex and violence" (Miller, Irving 159). It is the radicals and the prostitutes "with the perversions they represent" (Ibid) who function as anti-role models for the Berry children. Clearly, the radicals—not unlike the Ellen Jamesians and the misogynists in *Garp* represent the 'contemporary fascist spirit'—and moreover they find themselves in bad faith, which becomes clear when the Berry family is taken hostage by them:

> "And after we blow up the Opera," Ernst said, "after we destroy an institution that the Viennese worship to the *disgusting* extreme that they worship their coffeehouses—that they worship the *past*—well . . . after we blow up the Opera, we'll have possession of an American family. We'll have an American family as hostage. And a *tragic* American family, too. The mother and the youngest child already victims of an accident. Americans love accidents. They think disasters are *neat*. And here we have a father struggling to raise his four surviving children, and we'll have them all *captured*."
>
> Father didn't follow this very well, and Franny asked Ernst, "What are your *demands?* If we're hostages, what are the demands?"
>
> "No demands, dead," Schwanger said.
>
> "We demand nothing," said Ernst, patiently—ever patiently. "We'll already have what we want. When we blow up the Opera and we have you as our *prisoners*, we'll already have what we want."
>
> "An audience," Schwanger said, almost in whisper.
>
> "Quite a wide audience," Ernst said. "An international audience. Not just a European audience, not just the *Schlagobers* and blood audience, but an *American* audience, too. The whole world will listen to what we have to say."
>
> "About *what?*" Freud asked. He was whispering, too.
>
> "About everything," Ernst said, so logically. "We'll have an audience for everything we've got to say—about everything." (Hotel 327)

Ernst is "a pornographer willing to murder and maim—not for a *cause*, which would be stupid enough, but for an *audience*" (Hotel

327), he takes on the role of a terrorist, in existentialist terms. He "lives" for an audience, just like the Sartrean waiter. It is also Ernst, who provides the larger context for the modern world's absurdity, as his character allows for a link between terrorism, violence and rape—two of whose victims, Franny and Susie, are taken hostage. John in his function as narrator equals terrorism with pornography:

> Ernst loved his pornography; Ernst worshiped the means. It is never the ends that matter—it is *only* the means that matter. The terrorist and the pornographer are in it *for* the means. The means is everything to them. The blast of the bomb, the elephant position, the *Schlagobers* and blood—they love it all. Their intellectual detachment is a fraud; their indifference is feigned. They both tell lies about having "higher purposes." A terrorist *is* a pornographer. (Hotel 330)

Rape completes a triplet of absurdity and bad faith, when we consider that a rapist "terrorizes another person solely 'for the means'" (Reilly 83-84), too.

The fairy tale aspect of the novel also clearly exemplifies the process of becoming able to live purposeful in an absurd world. It is thus unsurprising that Miller (Irving 129-130) would argue that the "novel concentrates on the maturation process, pursuing its characters only to the threshold of adulthood, highlighting the experiences and the discovery of identity necessary to the attainment of that state." Essentially, the novel thus addresses—to a higher degree as is the case in Irving's other novels—the three central fairy tale questions defined by Bettelheim: What is the world really like? How am I to live my life in it? How can I truly be myself? (cf. Miller, Irving 131-132). The life stories of the novels' characters subsequently have to be seen as a struggle to find "strategies for coping with life, and to indicate the possibilities of success in the struggle for selfhood" (Ibid). Not unintentionally has Irving chosen the three hotels to correspond to the three fairy tale stages of separation, initiation and return. In reference to the *Bildungsroman*-like structure of the novel, Thunecke notes in this context that "after their return to New York in 1964, and as a result

68

from their experience abroad, the Berry children—or at least three of them, Lilly, the novelist being the exception—seem better prepared for the hostile US world of the mid-1960s" (287). From an existentialist perspective, these observations correspond perfectly well to the existentialist's struggle in finding meaning and individual values, being confronted with the outer world.

As is the case with the other two Irving novels, the analysis at hand deals with, the remedy against an absurd life in *The Hotel New Hampshire* is granted by the family unit. Particularly the first Hotel New Hampshire, provides "a protective, womblike place, a haven where the children feel comfortable and secure from the dangers of a cold, loveless world outside" (Miller, Irving 132). Particularly striking is the fact that the family remains close throughout the novel, and DeMott (13) argues in this context that "the sympathy and solidarity of the family members are in evidence—qualities placing the Berrys firmly in a world of light and affirmation." The absurd and violent world, which we have encountered in *Garp* as the Under Toad, in *Hotel* takes the form of the above mentioned dog Sorrow. The key to "achieve a true and lasting identity, establishing a strong personality in the struggle against the impersonal forces of death and destruction which menace this life" (Miller, Irving 130) is to understand this Sorrow in order to counteract it.

Coming to terms with Irving's Under Toad and overcoming—transcending—it, is exemplified by specific occasions in the novel. Franny, for example, after having been gang raped by members of the Dairy School's football team, most notably by Chipper Dove, is bound to change her perception of sexuality. Although holding on to the thought that the rape could not destroy her the "me in me," it is clear that the rape cast a dark shadow on her existence, which becomes clear when considering her taking three baths a day. However, Franny is able to transcend her exposure to violence and sex when she overhears her parents making love:

> They [the parents] have to use the hotel," Franny said, "just to get away from *us!*"
> I couldn't see what she was thinking.

"God!" Franny said. "They really *love* each other—they really *do!*"

And I wondered why I had taken such a thing for granted, and why it seemed to surprise my sister so much. Franny dropped my hand and wrapped her arms around herself; she hugged herself, as if she were trying to wake herself up, or get warm. "What am *I* going to do?" she said. "What's it going to be like? What happens next?" she asked.

[...]

"You were going to take a bath," I reminded Franny, who seemed in need of reminding—or some other advice.

"What?" she said.

"A bath," I said. "*That's* what was going to happen next. You were going to take a bath."

"Ha!" Franny cried. "The hell with that!" she said. "Fuck the bath!" said Franny, and went on hugging herself, and moving in place, as if she were trying to dance with herself. (Hotel 132)

Although Franny is in the process of overcoming her rape, she still finds herself struggling with being drawn to the dark side, which becomes apparent in her involvement with Ernst the radical and pornographer. At an earlier stage we already learned that although thinking of themselves as "normal and nice", "the children's sprightly R-rated obscenities decorate virtually every paragraph" (DeMott 14). The obscene and the dark thus accompany the Berry children and they are surely not "untouched by deviance" (Ibid). It is not surprising thus that Franny engages in a lesbian love affair with Susie and finds herself in love with her younger brother John. Nonetheless, her complicated emotional life provides a route to salvation from her penchant for the dark. Thus, her romantic relationship with Susie—who had been raped as well—can be seen as just another step in both women's healing processes. On the one hand, Susie is able to help Franny to acknowledge her rape and lectures "Franny about the need to be angry about her experience and to deal with it actively" (Miller, Irving 158). On the other hand, Franny provides Susie with "confidence in herself, encouraging her sense of self-worth" (Ibid) through their homosexual relationship. In an existentialist light, Susie's development in this respect is particularly revealing when considering the dimension of being-for-others. When Susie had been raped, the rapist had put a bag over her head, which led Susie to the assumption that she was the "original not-bad-if-you-put-a-bag-over-her-head-girl." Susie had been made "ugly" by the rapist and her subsequently being ashamed of her ugliness prompted her to wear a bear suit. After her involvement with Franny there is no more use for a bear-suit, as Franny had "gazed" upon her differently and thus was able to restore Susie's self-confidence.

The final liberation from both—Franny's rape and the infatuation of John and Franny—occurs in New York. It is in the Big Apple that Franny and John finally sleep together in order to overcome their incestuous passion in order to "release" (Hotel 355) themselves into their own lives. They can achieve this by having sex "beyond the point of exhaustion and to the point of physical pain" (Campbell 93). Moreover, this incestuous act serves as another "means of canceling the memory of the cruel rape" (DeMott 15). The ultimate catharsis for Franny, that will allow her to open up towards a life of health, procreation and marriage with Junior Jones, occurs when the Berry children and Susie manage to terrify Chipper Dove with the prospect of being raped by a bear (Ibid 13), who will at last have to realize that he must alter his sexist ways. And since Irving has created a world, in which everything can happen (Miller, Irving 135), it is not surprising that after the incestuous encounter with his sister, John is also able to transcend into a healthy relationship with Susie.

Frank, the homosexual child in the family, too, is able to redefine his existence. His encounter with Vienna allows him to transcend everyday morality—he had been the victim of harassment in the United States due to his homosexuality—and accept himself truly. In being confronted with an absurd Viennese world, where Frank studies the city's history, he turns into a "near-violent atheist" (Hotel 240), who in a truly postmodern manner rejects beliefs of all kinds and readily "adjusts to his homosexuality" (Reilly 86):

> As a result of Sorrow's tricking him [death of Mother and Egg, while flying with the dog he had stuffed], Frank would come down very hard on *belief* of any kind. He would become a greater

nonbeliever than Franny or me. A near-violent atheist, Frank would turn to believing only in Fate—in random fortune or random doom, in arbitrary slapstick and arbitrary sorrow. He would become a preacher *against* every bill of goods anyone ever sold: from politics to morality, Frank was always the opposition. (Hotel 240-241)

His maturation as an existentialist personae per se can be seen in the fact that he becomes the caretaker of the family. Having studied economics and realizing the potential of the younger sister Lilly as a writer, he becomes her agent and keeps the family financially secure. He in fact is the manifestation of the family's mantra "keep passing the open window," alluding to the folktale *The King of Mice*, where an unhappy Viennese performer "one day quit 'passing the open windows'" (Campbell 92) and committed suicide. Yet, Frank carries on, is poised against all possible adversity (Miller, Irving 162), and his redefinition can ultimately be seen as truly existentialist.

From another angle, Freud, too, makes himself an existentialist hero of a high degree. Having been blinded in a Nazi death camp experiment, Freud presents himself to be "properly proud" (Miller, Irving 157) of having outsmarted death:

> "Right here!" Freud screamed, stamping and whacking with the baseball bat. "Describe the plaque to me!" he cried. "I've never seen it."
> Of course: because it was in one of the camps that he went blind.
> They had performed some failed experiment on his eyes in the camp.
> "No, not *summer* camp," Franny had to tell Lilly, who had always been afraid of being sent to summer camp and was unsurprised to hear thet they tortured the campers.
> "Not *summer* camp, Lilly," Frank saud. "Freud was in a *death* camp."
> "But Herr Tod never found me," Freud said to Lilly. "Mr. Death never found me at home when he called." (Hotel 269)

Freud's attitude towards the probably most grotesque, violent and absurd experience a person could encounter, thus must be seen as a "celebration of the life force over death" (Miller, Irving 158). Considering Camus' statement that there "is no fate that cannot be surmounted by scorn" (Camus 117), it is not surprising that Freud becomes a role model for the Berrys who have to deal with their own losses.

In the final chapter, it becomes once more clear that Irving's version of solidarity in an absurd world, can be regarded existentialist. Although Father never actually can achieve his dream of successfully running a hotel, his dream still comes true through his children. Having made a fortune out of Lilly's writing, John and Susie run the third Hotel New Hampshire as a successful rape crisis center, and thus the children "metaphorically become 'caretakers' of their father's illusions" (Reilly 84).

> And my father has his illusions; they are powerful enough. My father's illusions are *his* good, smart bear—at last. And that leaves me, of course, with Susie the bear—with her rape crisis center and my fairy-tale hotel—so I'm alright, too. You have to be all right if you're expecting a baby.
> Coach Bob knew it all along: you've got to get obsessed and stay obsessed. You have to keep passing the open windows. (Hotel 419)

It is not surprising that DeMott would conclude that "we intuit that this work (when the grotesque heaves into sight) is not only about the unbearable but about our instinct for refusing the unbearable—not only about the worst of life but about our capacity for willing away the worst" (15).

4. Conclusion

At this point, it is time to return to the central point of this analysis, which assumes that the protagonists in John Irving's novels *The Water-Method Man*, *The World According to Garp* and *The Hotel New Hampshire* can be regarded existentialist heroes. The central criteria for an truly existentialist lifestyle have been defined in chapter 2.3., but shall be recaptured in a nutshell at this point. The starting point for an existentialist attitude is most certainly the individual's recognition of the world as absurd. An existentialist hero will then try to find meaning in the world, but come to the conclusion that metaphysics cannot provide satisfactory answers. However, he will know one thing for sure: that one's individual existence in absurdity is not a singular event, but rather that everyone else is facing absurdity too. Instead of falling into despair and mourning life's obvious meaninglessness, the existential hero becomes a rebel against the absurd and himself gives meaning to his life. Salvation can only be found through human solidarity and thus our hero will reach out to others. In the context of human coexistence, however, the existentialist exploit is to reject everyday morality and define his own values. Moreover, authenticity is the defining element for an existentialist hero's integrity, identity and dignity. Thus a truly existentialist individual will only accept views others have of himself, if they reflect his own concept of his identity. This subsequently implies that an existentialist hero, will also handle the mechanisms of masochism and sadism well to some degree, or at least be aware of it and learn his lesson.

As should have become more than just clear in the course of this analysis, all protagonists in Irving's discussed novels, deal excessively with the world's absurdity. Bogus Trumper can hardly deal with his existence in such a hostile place and regards it as threatening in every possible way. Not only does he see his own existence in this light, but has a hard time with his son Colm's and even with a mouse's vulnerability. The deaths in *The World According to Garp* appear to be random and absurd—whether it is the Fletchers' plane that crashes on a flight into the Caribbean, or whether it is the obscure car crash Walt dies in. Jenny Fields and Garp both die on the watch of people who blame others for their wretched conditions, never reaching a state of real consciousness—it is Pooh Percy and the unhappily divorced New Hampshire deer hunter who represent the existentialist anti-heroes. In *The World According to Garp* and *The Hotel New* Hampshire, rape is both a strong representation of the world's hostility and the absence of any values and morals. Moreover, the rapist who interferes and violates another individual's life course and psyche is the archetype of the existentialist anti-hero in Irving's work. Instead of revolting against the absurd through solidarity with others, the rapist indulges and confirms hostility. In *The Hotel New Hampshire* rape becomes emblematic for the cruel post-World War II world. Rape, the killing of a bear, the Holocaust all stand for a cruel new world in which sorrow dictates people's life. For the Berrys 'Sorrow' is brought into the family by exactly this name. And they encounter sorrow everywhere—in plane crashes, in a hotel inhabited by terrorists, in Freud who survived the Holocaust, and in encountering a 1950s Vienna which resembles an abandoned battlefield. As Shostak notes: "Not surprisingly, many of the motifs and 'litanies' [...] emerge from [Irving's] essential perception of the contained and uncontained dangers of the world, its physical and moral violence; the meaning of Irving's narratives is the 'lunacy and sorrow' that Garp's biographer identifies when he titles his book about Garp" (Repetition 103).

Most of Irving's characters thus try to extract meaning from what they experience in the dangerous and absurd world, which is logical, given that "the existential attitude is first of all an attitude of self-consciousness" (Solomon, Hegel to Existentialism 239). Bogus Trumper poses the big question of how everything is related to everything else. His neurotic mind in the end has to facilitate writing as a tool to approach the penultimate question of who he really is. And also thus Garp: starting out with the pretense to write about "what he has to say" (Irving, Garp 35), Garp soon has to realize that there are clear limitations to knowledge about the world. However, his truly existentialist experiences in Vienna allow for him to get his "scheme of things." This scheme—not explicit knowledge about "things"—reoccurs in *The Hotel New Hampshire*, where a fundamental understanding of "sorrow" becomes a tool against it, enabling the individual to "keep passing open windows"—the ability to not despair in tragedy and to scorn and thus overcome one's fate.

Irving's characters moreover clearly rebel against the absurdity they are facing. Bogus Trumper will not allow for Biggie to be successful in her endeavor to kill a defenseless rodent in their Iowa basement. He follows Colm—hiding behind bushes—just to see that he is well and alive, and not hit by a car. Irving's characters thus act against the world's hostility in solidarity. Jenny Fields opens her Dogshead Harbor estate to abused women in need of help—very prominent victims of this hostile world. Garp cannot do anything else but to catch the rapist of a young girl in a park (in existentialism it is also the things that we do not do that define our integrity). Wrestling becomes a preparation for life—chosen by a mother for her son. Moreover, we learn that Charlotte—the dying and aging Viennese prostitute—shows Garp, becoming somewhat like a spiritual mistress—that one can laugh at death and keep one's pride. Mastery of the existentialist scorning of one's fate is achieved by Freud, who although having been blinded in a Nazi concentration camp, thinks of himself as someone who has succeeded in outsmarting death. Never surrendering, and attributing life as something positive despite its absurdity becomes apparent with all characters—except for Lilly who commits suicide because she cannot "grow" enough. Even when the Garp's son Walt dies, the characters succeed in maintaining a "positive code for life" and they demonstrate this by deciding to have another child—Jenny Garp. What else could be more life affirming?! Rebellion against the absurd as an issue of communality probably is best represented in Irving's work through the closeness of families. Irving's families—no matter whether the Garps or the Berrys—will stick together through thick and thin, never forgetting about their individual fights against absurdity. Only when people are together who are not supposed to be together—most prominently Bogus Trumper and Biggie—will we find real human distance.

John Irving's existentialist heroes cannot appreciate everyday morality at all—they transcend common morals and create their own values. For Jenny Fields it would have been—due to her New England upper-class upbringing—only logical to summon a "suitable" profession. Instead she chooses to become a nurse; clearly a déclassé profession for the offspring of a wealthy WASP family. Jenny Fields, thus remains faithful to herself and avoids falling into bad faith. We also find deeds that would not be accepted by a larger society, but they are revealing in terms of an existentialist analysis. Frank and Franny in *Hotel New Hampshire* are aware of their "incestuous passion" for each other, but they still do not shy back from it. In order to transcend their 'problem,' they have to make love over and over again, until no one involved can imagine repeating this act ever again. From an existentialist perspective there are no excuses—Frank and Franny go straight into the core of the 'problem' and resolve it. Since life is also the things we do not do, their sexual encounter can be seen as something courageous; who knows what could have happened otherwise. Sexuality has thus a positive connotation attached to itself in Irving's work. For Garp sex has become an "act of terrific optimism" following his first sexual encounter with Cushie Percy. Yet, most of Irving's characters engage heavily in this form of "optimism," as has already been seen with Franny and Frank not stepping back from incest. Lust is at hand in *The Water-Method Man*, although Bogus Trumper actually never becomes the Camusean Don Juan. He remains in a state of lusting for Lydia Kindle, never actually cheating on Biggie, which seems to be due to his not yet overcoming everyday morality—which can be seen in the fact that his subconscious exposes him as a "prick" for even thinking of engaging with Lydia Kindle. Garp, on the other hand, comes pretty close to being a Camusean Don Juan; prostitutes, babysitters, and partner exchange are on his "sexual menu." It to some extent seems to keep Garp happy if he can have his meaningless flings. Upon meeting the Fletchers, Helen joins Garp in "sexual optimism," establishing an out of the ordinary "quaternation" (Reilly 65). However, soon the partner switching leads to existential sadism and masochism. Helen realizes that she "suffered the most"

(Ibid 68) and the four people involved quit the arrangement. Thus we can conclude, that Garp and Helen are mature enough to be aware of the traps laid out by being-for-others and consequently act accordingly. This once more becomes apparent when Helen quits an affair later with her student Michael Milton, as soon as she realizes having hurt her husband. Bogus Trumper, on the other hand, is not aware of his own sadism towards Biggie.

How sane a change in morality can be is exemplified by Frank's time in Vienna. It is his experience with the world's absurdity in Vienna that liberates him. With an air of the absurd, Frank's homosexuality becomes something plainly normal and acceptable, and he no longer has to remain a homosexual in the closet. Vienna, plays a significant role in terms of values in another of Irving's novels, too. Garp who has bonded with Charlotte and who had gotten his "scheme of things" does not have a problem pretending to be Charlotte's son when he goes to see her in the hospital. Accepting people in their humanity and who they really are—not what they represent in the context of morality—thus appears to be a central point in Irving's narrative.

Being-for-others surfaces many times in all three novels. Trumper, for example who technically did not cheat on his wife, nevertheless is regarded as a cheater by Biggie. This corresponds perfectly well with Trumper's malaise with who he really is. As Tulpen suggests, nobody *knows* Trumper, not even himself. Being-for-others, being "gazed upon," most prominently shows in the figure of Jenny Fields. She knows who she is: a strong woman, doing the right thing. Immediately, however, her environment and the world start to see her as the personified feminist. Jenny Fields; by not giving in to "being" the feminist the world sees in her, she avoids taking on a role and thus does not commit the existentialist "mistake" of falling into bad faith; she remains what she is: a nurse. The tension between her being-for-itself and her being-for-others is maintained throughout the novel. Some characters in the novels, however, actually fall into bad faith: namely the Ellen Jamesians and the Viennese radicals. The Ellen Jamesians, on the one hand—besides being a caricature of themselves—define their existence through a distorted version of radical feminism that has become a plain and simple ideology. A cut out tongue becomes everything to them—"to the exclusion of everything else" (79), as Campbell sees their role in the novel. The radicals, on the other hand, are terrorists not for a cause but for an audience as becomes clear in the dialogue, when the Berrys are held hostages. Playing a role without any purpose is a striking example of bad faith, and reminds very much of the caricature of the Parisian waiter Sartre has provided.

Returning to the tension between the being-for-itself and the being-for-others, we encounter such frictions also in the close relationships of the protagonists, portrayed in *Garp*. Although they are—as noted above—close to each other, they are always aware of a tension between themselves and other people. Thus, even in times of betrayal and disappointments the protagonists connect deeply. The enormous impact of being-for-others can be seen in the masquerade of Susie the Bear in *The Hotel New Hampshire*. By putting a bag over head, while raping her, her rapist 'succeeded' in making her believe in her ugliness. Only when Franny engages erotically with Susie, will the soon-to-be-former-bear begin to appreciate herself as somebody beautiful again. *Hotel New Hampshire* also plays with being-for-others, portraying the novel's anti-heroes in their being-for-others, their "being-for-us-the-reader." Thus names such as Schwanger ('pregnant'), Fehlgeburt ('miscarriage') or Arbeiter ('worker') in the end are not surprising in an existentialist literary perspective.

The ability to transcend—from one's facticity—is also aptly portrayed by Irving throughout all the novels. In *The Water-Method Man*, Trumper has to learn that freedom does not mean being able to act irresponsibly, but rather that one is free to commit oneself to what is really important. Thus Trumper has to down his "freedom" from commitments and stop making excuses. Garp, in the end manages to overcome his weak spot: intolerance toward the intolerant. Garp develops understanding for the Ellen Jamesians, but at this point Irving's absurdity strikes again, and he has Garp killed by the hands of Pooh Percy, an Ellen Jamesian. In order to keep faith in each other, the protagonists also have to develop their own values systems, but they can only do so through experience. Garp will at some point discover that faithfulness is a practical tool in working towards a happy relationship, Trumper accepts that commitment is a key to success and stability. Also, the protagonists in Irving's novels succeed in changing their perceptions. Even Franny, with her horrible rape experience starts to rethink her stance on sexuality—which is linked to brute violence—and gets excited when she overhears her parents making love, realizing that sexuality can actually be something positive.

Although several scholars, among them Reilly, Harter and Thompson, and Miller (cf. chapter three) have briefly referenced existentialist factors in analyzing Irving's work, to date none has utilized existentialism as the major analytical framework for such an analysis.

The aim of this analysis is to demonstrate that existentialism can provide a viable framework to help us better understand and analyze Irving's novels. Clearly, many of Irving's protagonists can be seen as existentialist heroes, and some of Irving's plots can be regarded as protagonists' stories of existentialist self-exploration. Within the context of the proposed existentialist framework, this analysis has examined three of Irving's novels.

5. Works Cited

Arrington, Robert L. A Companion to the Philosophers. Malden, MA et al: Blackwell, 1999.

Aurelius, Marcus: Meditations. London: Penguin, 1964.

Bowers Hill, Jane. "John Irving's Aesthetics of Accessibility." John Irving. Ed. Harold Bloom. Philadelphia, PA: Chelsea House Publishers, 2001. 65-72.

Brée, Germaine. Albert Camus. Gestalt und Werk. Reinbek: Rowohlt, 1960.

Bruneau, Jean. "Existentialism and the American Novel." Yale French Studies 1 (1948). 66-72.

Campbell, Josie P. John Irving. A Critical Companion. Westport, CT and London: Greenwood Press, 1998.

Camus, Albert. The Myth of Sisyphus. London: Penguin Books, 2005.

Davis, Todd F. and Kenneth Womack. The Critical Response to John Irving. Westport, CT and London: Praeger, 2004.

DeMott, Benjamin. "Domesticated Madness." John Irving. Ed. Harold Bloom. Philadelphia, PA: Chelsea House Publishers, 2001. 11-18.

Des Pres, Terence. "Review of The World According to Garp." The New Republic 29 (1978): 31-33.

Epstein, Joseph. "Why John Irving Is So Popular." Commentary 73.6 (1982): 59-63.

Freeland, Alison. "A Conversation with John Irving." New England Review: Middlebury Series 18.2 (1997): 135-142.

French, Marylin. "The Garp Phenomenon." The Critical Response to John Irving. Ed. Davis, Todd F. and Kenneth Womack. Westport, CT: Praeger, 2004, 74-78.

Friedl, Herwig and Dieter Schulz. "A Multiplicity of Witness: E. L. Doctorow at Heidelberg." Conversations with E. L. Doctorow. Ed. Christopher D. Morris. Jackson: University Press of Mississippi, 1999, 112-128.

Greil, Marcus. "Garp: Death in the Family." John Irving. Ed. Harold Bloom. Philadelphia, PA: Chelsea House Publishers, 2001. 3-10.

—— "John Irving: The World of the World According to Garp." Rolling Stone 306 (1979): 68-75.

Harter, Carol C. and James R. Thompson. John Irving. Boston, MA: Twayne Publishers, 1986.

Irving, John. The Hotel New Hampshire. New York: Ballantine Books, 1995.

—— The Water-Method Man. New York: Ballantine Books, 1990.

—— The World According to Garp. New York: Ballantine Books, 1997.

Klinkowitz, Jerome. "John Irving's World According to Fiction." The Critical Response to John Irving. Ed. Davis, Todd F. and Kenneth Womack. Westport, CT: Praeger, 2004, 43-56.

McBride, William L. Sartre's Life, Times, and Vision Du Monde. New York: Garland, 1997.

McCaffery, Larry. "An Interview with John Irving." Contemporary Literature 23.1 (1982): 1-18.

Macann, Christopher. Four Phenomenological Philosophers. Husserl, Heidegger, Sartre, Merleau-Ponty. London et al: Routledge, 1999.

Miller, Gabriel. "The Good Wrestler." John Irving. Ed. Harold Bloom. Philadelphia, PA: Chelsea House Publishers, 2001. 49-64.

—— John Irving. New York, NY: Ungar, 1982.

Murdoch, Iris. "De Beauvoir's The Ethics of Ambiguity." Existentialists and Mystics. Ed. Peter Conradi. London: Chatto & Windus, 1997. 122-124.

——— "Existentialists and Mystics." Existentialists and Mystics. Ed. Peter Conradi. London: Chatto & Windus, 1997. 221-234.

——— "The Existentialist Hero." Existentialists and Mystics. Ed. Peter Conradi. London: Chatto & Windus, 1997. 108-115.

——— "Vision and Choice in Morality." Existentialists and Mystics. Ed. Peter Conradi. London: Chatto & Windus, 1997. 76-98

Priestley, Michael. "An Interview with John Irving." New England Review 1 (1979): 489-504.

——— "Structure in the Worlds of John Irving." John Irving. Ed. Harold Bloom. Philadelphia, PA: Chelsea House Publishers, 2001. 19-32.

Rickard, John. "Wrestling with the Text: The World According to John Irving." Meanjin 56.3-4 (1997): 714-722.

Sagi, Abraham. Albert Camus and the Philosophy of the Absurd. Amsterdam: Rodopi, 2002.

Sartre, Jean-Paul. Basic Writings. Ed. Stephen Priest. London: Routledge, 2001.

——— Being and Nothingness. New York et al: Washington Square, 1993.

——— Existentialism and Humanism. London: Methuen, 1966.

Shostak, Debra. "Plot as Repetition: John Irving's Narrative Experiments." The Critical Response to John Irving. Ed. Davis, Todd F. and Kenneth Womack. Westport, CT: Praeger, 2004, 101-117.

——— "The Family Romances of John Irving." John Irving. Ed. Harold Bloom. Philadelphia, PA: Chelsea House Publishers, 2001. 87-104.

Solomon, Robert C. "Introduction." Phenomenology and Existentialism. Ed. Robert C. Solomon. Lanham, MD: Rowman & Littlefield, 2001

—— From Hegel to Existentialism. Oxford et al: Oxford University Press, 1987.

—— The Passions. Emotions and the Meaning of Life. Indianapolis, IN: Hackett, 1993.

Suhr, Martin. Jean Paul Sartre. Zur Einführung. Hamburg: Junius, 2004.

Thunecke, Jörg. "Schlagobers and Blood: Vienna in John Irving's Novel The Hotel New Hampshire." Austria in Literature. Ed. Donald G. Daviau. Riverside, CA: Ariadne, 2000. 276-294.

Towers, Robert. "Reservations." John Irving. Ed. Harold Bloom. Philadelphia, PA: Chelsea House Publishers, 2001. 33-38.

Wilson, Raymond. "The Postmodern Novel: The Example of John Irving's The World According to Garp." Critique: Studies in Contemporary Fiction 34.1 (1992): 49-62.

Zima, Peter V. Der gleichgültige Held. Stuttgart: Metzler, 1983.

16911014R10052

Printed in Great Britain
by Amazon